D0556866

THE RETURN

I was deep in dreamless sleep. Then, suddenly awake, I was aware of the dark room, touched only by the faint glimmer of light at the window. I sat up, knowing that there had been a faint noise nearby . . .

I listened and heard nothing. I waited, straining to hear, for what seemed endless time but could only have been a minute or two. Then, just as I was about to dismiss the sound as imagined, I heard it again.

A faint click, a purr. The jostle of metal against metal. The small elevator was in use again.

Who had touched the controls?

Who was stealthily riding in the small metal cage . . . ?

Avon Books by
Daoma Winston

MOORHAVEN	14126	$1.50
EMERALD STATION	18200	$1.50
THE INHERITANCE	20701	$1.25

DAOMA WINSTON
THE RETURN

AVON
PUBLISHERS OF BARD, CAMELOT, DISCUS, EQUINOX AND FLARE BOOKS

AVON BOOKS
A division of
The Hearst Corporation
959 Eighth Avenue
New York, New York 10019

ISBN: 0-380-00311-2

First Avon Printing, February, 1972
Third Printing

AVON TRADEMARK REG. U.S. PAT. OFF. AND
FOREIGN COUNTRIES, REGISTERED TRADEMARK—
MARCA REGISTRADA, HECHO EN CHICAGO, U.S.A.

Printed in the U.S.A.

For Mike and Ruth Mosettig

THE RETURN

1

I NEVER REALIZED until the moment I faced the imminent possibility of death, and felt its cold mist swirl around me, that I had lived all my life in a protracted dream. I learned unquestioning acceptance early, and took for granted that lonely existence against which others might have rebelled. Even so, there were within me all those bright expectations of love and happiness that every young girl has. It was as if I were sleeping, awaiting only to be awakened. But what awakened me was terror. . . .

It began in the most simple and innocent fashion.

I was sitting at my desk in the big, light gleaming room.

A shadow fell over my typewriter. A sweet, husky voice said, "Hi, Gaby. How are you getting on?"

I let my hands drop from the keys, and looked up with pleased surprise.

I had been working for Case Life and Casualty Company for three months, and this was the first time anyone had paid any attention to me at all, much less bothered to learn and call me by my first name. It was always, "Miss Tysson, are the blank blank forms ready?" Or, "Miss Tysson, I'll need these this afternoon."

The building loomed sixteen stories high above the busy street, concrete and glass and chrome occupying half of a city block. When I had first seen it I thought of it as a giant beehive, and of myself as a lonely bee creeping in with hopes of finding a cell in which to settle safely. In my time there, the fancy had been reenforced. At nine in the morning, the bees swarmed in. At five in the evening they swarmed out. From the hive they took their sustenance and protection, but it was an impersonal and meaningless place, a microcosm of the world as I knew it then.

"Don't you remember me?" the sweet, husky voice was demanding.

I grinned into the glowing green eyes that looked down at me. "Of course I do. You work in Personnel."

"Exactly. But I'll bet you don't know my name."

My grin widened, stretching my lips. I said, "You're Jessie Davis."

I could have said, and truthfully, too, that I supposed nobody who had ever met Jessie Davis would forget her, or her name. She was a woman in her late twenties, a striking redhead with exotic green eyes. The first time I had seen her she wore a lime green pants suit and sat behind a big mahogany desk, her long white fingers delicately handling application forms. She had seemed a goddess to me—assured,

THE RETURN **11**

successful, with the world at her command. She was the kind of woman I would like to have been, long-legged and lithe and controlled to a sophisticated perfection. But I knew that I could wish all I wanted —I would never be another Jessie Davis. I was too short, and my· curly blonde hair was too undisciplined. My brown eyes were too wide open and eager, and my face, with its exaggerated dimples, was more pixie than person.

Now Jessie said, "I've been meaning for ages to come down from upstairs, to see how you were getting along."

"Oh, I'm fine. It's nice here," I told her.

"Do you like the work?"

"Of course." I tried to put enthusiasm into my voice. I didn't really enjoy the filling in of multiple forms hour after hour. But I didn't intend to perhaps jeopardize my job by telling Jessie Davis that. "It's interesting," I added hopefully.

Jessie's red mouth turned down. Her slim shoulders shrugged within the lavender blouse she wore. "Nonsense, you know you're totally bored. You're much too clever to be stuck with this kind of thing." Her slim white fingers tapped the typewriter. "And you won't be I'm sure. Just give it time. I have my eyes on you, Gaby." She glanced at her tiny jeweled watch. "It's two minutes to twelve, Gaby. I think you can come and have lunch with me."

My eyes shifted in a quick doubtful glance to the other four girls in the room.

Jessie laughed softly. "I don't think you need to worry about them, do you?"

That was the beginning.

I was two months away from my twenty-first

birthday, quite alone in the world since my mother's
death some five months before. I had lived in the
city since the age of ten, grown up and gone to
school there, but my mother and I had always lived
a very sheltered life. She had been possessive and
protective of me, and in the last few years she had
suffered a wasting illness that had made her very
dependent. Thus I had very few friends, and those
not close.

I was definitely uneasy when I went to lunch with
Jessie Davis that day. I couldn't imagine why she
would pay any attention to me. I couldn't picture
what we would talk about. I thought of myself as
dull, with neither wit nor charm, with no exciting
experiences to share, with no stories to tell.

But Jessie seemed to find me interesting enough.
Her green eyes glowed at me. Her tilted smile
warmed and relaxed me.

I found myself laughing as I hadn't laughed in a
long time at comments Jessie made, and joyfully
realized that Jessie laughed just as hard at what I
said in return.

We had lunch together several times that week,
and I began to look forward to those forty-five
minute breaks as by far the best part of my days.

But it was Jessie who said, "You know what,
Gaby? I want you to come to my place for dinner
tonight. Are you free? Or do you have a date with
some glamorous man that you've been keeping a
secret from me."

I did date several men, but none that qualified for
Jessie's description. I grinned, "I don't have any
secrets from you."

Jessie said "I'll bet you do." Then, "You'll come
tonight?"

"Of course," I promised. "But you have to let me take you out to dinner next week. I can't entertain you in my room. It's not up to guests, you know."

"Next week will take care of itself," Jessie retorted.

It was that evening, over candlelight, made drowsy by wine with which I had had little experience, that I heard myself telling Jessie about my childhood memories. Much later, trying to recall how the subject had been brought up, I could remember only that Jessie had said, "Sometimes I look back, and I get the feeling that I must have been born about the age of ten or twelve or something like that." She had grinned, "Maybe because it's part of the misty past literally. But very little before then sticks in my mind."

I had said thoughtfully, "It might be that way for everyone. I don't remember much of my life either before I was ten." I paused then, thinking about the cold, foggy night when my mother had come into the big, pale blue room that had formed much of my universe until then. I had been sleeping soundly. My mother awakened me with a touch. Tears were on her cheeks. She held me close and hard for a moment. Then she whispered, "We're leaving here, Gaby. I want you to dress now. I want you to hurry and dress, and be quiet. Be very, very quiet."

Dazed with fatigue—with shock, too, for it had been a long terrible day—I had obeyed.

We came to the city and stayed a few days in a hotel. Then we moved into a fourth floor walkup, where the garden had been converted to parking lots and the windows were always smeared with smog.

In the years that followed, my mother had never explained why we had slipped away from Cornell

House so soon after my father was buried. My mother never spoke of Cornell House again, nor the relatives that lived there. It was as if that time, those people, had never existed. Gradually they faded from my mind, the void to be filled with day-to-day experiences, and my mother's constant, anxious supervision.

Now, looking into Jessie's lovely face, I suddenly realized that she must be the same age that my mother was when she lost my father. She had been widowed so young, left so alone, with only me to love and depend on. I knew that was why she had always been so fearful, yet demanding—why she didn't really want me to have friends, to go out.

"But I remember where I lived," I found myself telling Jessie. "It was called Cornell House. It was a big place, set high on a steep mountainside. The ocean was at the foot of the cliffs, and there were wide, beautiful meadows, and a few horses and lots of dogs."

"It sounds lovely," Jessie said.

"It was," I agreed. But I was thinking of my father. He was tall, blond. He laughed a lot.

"Did you ride the horses?" Jessie was asking.

"We all did. My mother didn't care for it, though, and never went unless my father really teased her into it."

Jessie said, "I grew up on a farm. We were dirt poor. I was so glad when we lost it that I laughed for two weeks. But it sounds to me as if you were rich."

"Maybe. We might have been then. Children don't think that way. But if we were, it didn't last. After we came to the city we certainly didn't have much money."

"Why did you come?"

Again I thought of that night. I said slowly, "I guess I don't really know, Jessie. But my father had just died, you see." I paused then.

Jessie made a wordless sound of sympathy and regret, but her green eyes were sharp and knowing.

I said, "I suppose that's why we went away. My mother never talked about it. And you know how children are. After a while they forget. They just forget, that's all."

"Forget?" Jessie asked. "What do you mean?"

"Why . . . everything. Whatever's left behind, I suppose."

It had been that way with me. We'd left Cornell House, and gradually the memory of it, of Fernetta, and Sally and Bernard, of the others, had faded from my mind.

Jessie was saying, "I guess so. Sometimes, some children, but. . . ."

"Especially when there's no real reason to remember."

"Then you don't have any idea of what happened, do you?" she asked.

I shook my head thoughtfully, trying to consider a past that had suddenly begun to become real again. "I don't know what happened. If anything did. But it *is* funny, now that I think of it. . . ."

"What is?"

"The way we left." I paused. "You see, it was the night of my father's funeral. He died. He. . . ." My throat was suddenly dry, closed. I couldn't speak. I wished we hadn't gotten on the subject, but I didn't know how to change it.

I saw my father's coffin. I saw my mother's frantic face. I heard her shrill accusing voice, screaming, "No, no. It didn't happen. It couldn't have. Not that way. Not to Denby. I know. I know. It didn't happen that way." I heard the scurry of words around me.

"What about your father?" Jessie was asking now.

"He was thrown from his mount. Satan's Son. A big black stallion, rough but a good one. Yes. That's what it was. He had a riding accident, and died. And we went to the funeral with my Aunt Sally and my Uncle Bernard, and the rest of them, and then that night my mother awakened me, and got me dressed, and we went away."

"Funny," Jessie said. "I guess she didn't get along with her in-laws."

"I guess not," I agreed. "Some people don't, of course."

"What was your father's name, Gaby?"

"Denby. And my mother's was Rosalie."

Jessie grinned. "My folks were Mary and John. Do you think names make lives? Or lives make names? Or what?"

"Maybe a little of each," I suggested. "But I do know I wish I'd been named something shorter than Gabriella."

"It's beautiful," Jessie protested.

"Too elaborate," I said.

"Perhaps it is for Case Life and Casualty. But it wasn't too elaborate for Cornell House."

"That's long behind me," I told her.

She refilled my glass with the tart red wine. "Take more of this, Gaby, and we'll concentrate on the future."

"I'll be glad to," I smiled.

"The future." Jessie raised her glass in a toast. "May it always be as bright as it looks right now."

She leaned forward. "You have a birthday pretty soon, don't you?"

I nodded.

"And it's twenty-one, isn't it?"

I nodded again.

"That's a lovely year," Jessie said, her husky voice full of laughter. "It's the best, Gaby. We'll have to do something to make it really memorable."

I shook my head. As far as I was concerned, one birthday was much like another. We had always paid little attention to them since we'd come to the city.

"Oh, but we must," Jessie said. She leaned her chin on her folded hands. "Now let me think." She was quiet for a moment, and hummed faintly. Then she cried, "I know. I know. We'll have a party for you." She reared back, flinging up her head at my quick, negative headshake. "But we will, Gaby. Why not?" she demanded.

I said, "It's so sweet of you to think of it, Jessie. But I. . . ." I felt my cheeks burn. I was embarrassed to have to say it, but I knew that I must. I hurried on, "I hardly know anybody to invite. I'd feel so funny. I haven't been to a real party in so long . . . no really, Jessie, it just wouldn't. . . ."

"It's time you made your debut," Jessie said. "Just leave everything to me. I know lots of people to invite, people you ought to get to know anyway." She began to laugh. "Oh, it's the most marvelous idea. And I have a thought. . . ." She fluttered long black lashes at me. "Oh, yes, I've just . . . it will be a surprise."

"Jessie, no. . . ."

"I won't tell you what it is. You'll find out when the time comes." She jumped up, ran to her table.

She riffled some papers there. "Now where did I . . . oh, yes, here it is. The calendar. What's the exact date?"

I told it to her. "Not quite two months away, you see."

She frowned, tapped her teeth with a pointed finger nail. "That long? Oh, dear. I might not be in town then."

"Let's not worry about it," I told her, relieved and disappointed at the same time. I didn't really want her to give me a twenty-first birthday party, but it was exciting to think about all the same.

"Just hold on there," she said. Then her face brightened. "There's no law that says you have to celebrate your birthday right on your birthday. We'll just do it a month before. There's no real reason to wait."

"But it'll be too much trouble for you," I protested.

"No. No, it won't be. It's a marvelous idea. And wait until you find out what my surprise is." She made a quick note on the calendar, and said, "May eleventh then, one month to the day before your birthday. Now you just leave all the rest of it to me."

That night, for the first time I could remember, I dreamed of Cornell House. I saw the wide terraces, and the corral and stables. I saw the blue of the sky against the black of the jutting cliffs. I saw the great tipped rock that was called Lovers Leap. A sudden storm spilled thunder and lightning across the meadows. I awakened strangely gripped by an uneasiness I couldn't name.

In the next few weeks, Jessie and I had lunch together several times. She was gay, fun to be with. She made me feel interested, and interesting.

The night I took her out to dinner, repaying her hospitality though she protested that I needn't, she helped me choose the dress I would wear to her party. It was royal blue, a crisp, lightweight cotton with a scooped neck and a tiny waist and a great, full skirt that belled above my knees.

It had cost a bit more than I wanted to spend but Jessie had been insistent.

"It's just perfect for you," she cried. "And it looks just like a twenty-first birthday party dress. You only have it once so indulge yourself. You can save on something else. If you have to. Buy it, Gaby. You won't be sorry."

I didn't know then that some time, and not very far in the future, I would be sorry—for a great many things. I hesitated for just a moment, but I did love the dress. I loved the way it felt on me, the way it made me feel. I bought it, and then I wished the time away until I could appear at Jessie's apartment, wearing it in hope and joy.

I saw Jessie only briefly during the last few days before the party. She was plainly busy at work, and occupied with her mysterious plans.

The night finally came, and with it came the awful trepidations that the timid feel when called upon to meet a large group of strangers. I came out of the cloud of hope and joy with a terrible thud. All I wanted to do was hide in my room, crawl into bed, and stay there. I was fluttery with panic. But I couldn't disappoint Jessie. I forced myself to dress. The blue seemed to brighten my pale skin and deepen my dimples. The silver sandals made my legs seem longer, my waist narrower. Jessie had offered to have someone stop by for me, but I insisted that I would allow myself the unaccustomed luxury of a cab. When it stopped before her apartment, I was very nearly immobilized. I would have to walk into the flat, to walk into a sea of strangers alone. I wished now that I had insisted on inviting a few of the girls from the office. I had suggested it to Jessie, but Jessie's green eyes had grown contemptuous. She'd said, "Goodness no, Gaby. What on earth do we want those drones for?" It was an oblique reference, of course, to the fancy I'd confessed to her, the idea that Case Life and Casualty was a giant beehive, and the people who worked there no more than swarming bees. I hadn't been willing to confess that I needed those bees for reassurance, that I was myself a drone, and could never be anything more. I just said, "Well, I thought it might be nice...."

"Nonsense," Jessie retorted firmly. "I want you to meet my friends. You'll love them. And they'll love you. They'll give you a start on a real social life. And besides ... there's the surprise...."

So there would be no one, no one at all, that I knew, except Jessie, of course.

In spite of the blue dress, the silver slippers, I itched to be gone and away. I longed to creep back to my room and stay there. I didn't know then that I would spend many nights wishing that I had followed that intuition.

Instead I took a deep breath and squared my shoulders. I carefully and determinedly set a silver slipper on the first step, a silver slipper on the second step. I touched the dusty bannister lightly with my fingertips.

I moved slowly and unwillingly up the staircase to the second floor, and followed the plain trail laid down by music and laughter to Jessie's door.

I paused there to take another deep breath, to fix a careful smile on my lips.

The door flew open at my timid knock. Light, and louder music, and laughter flooded around me.

Something in me shrank back. Something in me whispered, "No, no. I can't do it. No. I don't want to be here."

Then Jessie came to meet me. She wore a buttercup yellow jumpsuit. Her red hair blazed in a long ponytail. Her green eyes glowed. She seized me, hugged me, drew me inside with her.

"Here she is, folks. Our birthday girl, Gaby Tysson!" she cried.

Pinned like a moth by the weight of all that concentrated attention, I searched beyond Jessie for another welcoming and friendly face, and suddenly met the deep, dark, smiling eyes of a man who stood waiting across the room.

2

HE WAS TALL, very lean, with wide shoulders relaxed into an easy slouch. His hair was dark, swept across his forehead in a single loose wave. His mouth was long and narrow, touched faintly now by the smile I saw in his deep set eyes.

He wore a white silk shirt, an expensively cut blue suit. There was a certain stillness about him, as if he had been patiently waiting for a long time.

For a moment our two glances met and held, and I felt so oddly drawn to him that I almost asked Jessie who he was. It seemed as if an inexplicable force had been set up between us when we exchanged looks. There was something just faintly familiar about him, as if I had seen him somewhere before. I thought it might have been in my dreams.

But then Jessie swept me into the group, crying, "Come on, everybody. Let's spread some names around."

There were about a dozen people there, each one of them as exciting and exotic as Jessie herself. Through the next hour she saw to it that I circulated among them, chatting timidly. Faces smiled at me. Hands gripped and dropped mine. I had my first taste of champagne, and whispered to Jessie, "You shouldn't have, Jess. It must have cost you a fortune."

"It's worth it," she retorted, "just to see the stars in your eyes."

But I had begun to feel that there couldn't be stars in my eyes. If my eyes were shining, it must be with tears. For an hour passed, then another. And I was aware, always, as I moved on the currents of the party, swirling with it from group to group, that the tall, dark young man remained across the room from me. He seemed to be the only one to whom I had not been introduced, who had not come forward to speak at least a few words to me. Only he, in whom I was most interested, had remained continually aloof.

I would have gone to him, but something held me back. Even the bubbling of champagne in me, the excitement of the party itself, didn't give me quite enough courage to act, though it gave me the courage to wish, to suppose that he might be as timid as I was myself.

Jessie had a high tiered birthday cake for me, and on it she had put candles. It had the place of honor, centered on the red cloth with white dishes around it. I admired it from a distance, thinking that was the surprise she had referred to.

But close to midnight Jessie appeared at my side frowning at her wristwatch. "Now where is she?"

"She?" I asked.

"Your surprise," Jessie grin   aven't you been wondering what happened

"I was too busy having a good time," I told her, and sneaked another quick, yearning look at the tall dark man across the room from us.

But Jessie's green eyes were sharp. She caught me at it. She said, "Oh, you've noticed him, have you?"

I didn't answer her.

She looked as if she were going to say more, but that was when the door opened.

A woman stood posing against the brightness and then swept in, bracelets and necklaces jangling. A long red skirt swayed around her sandaled feet. A tight black bodice fit her like a second skin, and over it she wore a fringed red shawl. Her eyes were deep set, black, and blindingly bright. Her long black hair lay in great wavy sheaves on her shoulders.

I knew then what my surprise was to be.

The woman was a Romany gypsy by the look of her. I was sure she had come to tell my fortune.

The room grew quiet as she came in. The laughter faded away. The clink of glasses was stilled.

Someone drew a deep, noisy breath.

She stopped before me, looked at me long and hard.

Jessie opened her lips as if to speak, but the gypsy shook her dark head. "No," she said. "No, no. You need not tell me. I am Drago. I know." Her hands settled on my shoulders, drew me close to her. Her brilliant eyes stared into my eyes, mesmerizing, hypnotizing. "You're Gaby Tysson," she said. Her voice was a husky drone. It came from lips that scarcely moved with the words. It was as if she were the vessel, as if the mind and voice that moved her were far away.

I wasn't sure that I liked being held and stared at. I moved restively, and looked across the room toward where the still smiling dark man stood. He was watching.

Drago recalled my attention with a small shake. "Have you never heard of Drago, the gypsy fortune teller?"

I shook my head.

"Come with me," Drago said. "We will go into a corner. I will tell you of the past, to prove my words. Then I will tell you of the future."

The room was suddenly swept with laughter again. There was music, and movement, and several couples danced in the center of the floor.

Drago smiled. "Surely you're not afraid."

"No," I faltered. "No, I'm not afraid." But that wasn't true. I was somehow frightened. I didn't want to know the future. I would learn it as it came. I didn't want my beautiful evening spoiled, perhaps. I didn't want to hear the sound of Drago's voice.

But I found myself seated in a corner. She sat directly in front of me, the light glinting on her earrings and necklaces, shining in her brilliant eyes.

She took my hand, stared at me, her scarlet lips moving without a sound.

At last she said, "There have been comings and goings. Yes, yes."

I instantly thought of Cornell House and how we had left there to come to the city.

She nodded. "There will be more of them. Not many. I see a journey, but that is later." She paused for a long moment. Then, "You have had sadness. A loss. No. Not one loss. You have had two. Each has changed your life, caused you suffering. Each has left you bereft."

I thought of my father's death, and what had happened. I thought of my mother's more recent death. Yes. Both times my life had been utterly changed.

"There was a beautiful place," she went on. "Much sunshine. The air was fresh and still over the changing colors of the ocean. Peace reigned. But then you were torn from there. You left roots behind. Those roots will flower."

I remembered Cornell House again.

Drago's smile broadened. She said, "You need never fear the future. It is good, good." She took my hand, looked into it. "I see love." A fingertip sketched a line of my palm. "I see a man. Handsome. Yes. A handsome man. As dark as you are fair. As tall as you are small."

My breath caught in my throat. My eyes shifted across the room to where the tall dark man stood talking with Jessie. Talking with Jessie, but I knew that he was still watching me. Jessie and he were about the same age and they looked good together, her red head tipped to his dark one.

Drago reclaimed my wandering attention. "Love, child. A tall dark man. And . . . oh, yes, wealth. Much wealth. A long life." She dropped my hand. "The future is all yours. Love, wealth, a long life."

"Thank you," I said. "It's a lovely fortune."

"A lovely future," she answered. "Follow your heart, Gaby Tysson. Follow your heart, and go where it leads, and you will never regret it."

It was then that Jessie came across the room, and with her was the tall dark man.

Drago drifted away, red skirt rustling, bracelets and necklaces jangling. She told a few more fortunes,

I noticed, and then she disappeared. I never saw her again the rest of the evening.

Jessie said, "Gaby, here's somebody that wants to meet you."

"I'm Benjamin Haley," the tall man said, and stopped expectantly, his dark brows rising in quizzical arches under the single wave that swept his forehead.

"Benjamin Haley," I said softly. "Benjamin . . . Ben. . . ."

At Cornell House there had been a tall dark man with a soft silky voice. Terrell Haley. There had been a boy, seventeen or eighteen—tall, too, and dark—I hadn't thought of them for years and years.

I said eagerly, "There's a part of my family that's named Haley. And there was a Benjamin. . . ."

He grinned, "Oh, Gaby, have I really changed all that much in these ten years? I knew you instantly. I thought it was so weird that we should find each other again this way."

"Benjamin . . . yes, of course. You're Benjamin."

"Do you really remember me now?"

"You've changed some," I admitted. "You're bigger and taller, and. . . ."

"I'm an old man now? Is that what you're trying to say?"

"Hardly," I answered. "If anything I've caught up to you."

Jessie cut in. "What's this all about?" she demanded. "What do you both mean?"

"We're very distant cousins," Benjamin told her. "For which, I might add right now, I am very glad." He bent a smiling glance on me, then returned his attention to Jessie. "When Gaby was a child—until she was about ten years old I'd guess—we lived together. Or rather we lived on the same property. Cornell House it was called. Hasn't she ever told you about it? Anyway, she lived in the main house with her parents and her Uncle Bernard and Aunt Sally. I stayed with my folks in what was called the cottage."

Terrell, and yes, Johanna. These were Benjamin's parents. The tall, silky voiced man. The slim, quiet woman. . . . I recalled them clearly now. A peculiar chill went over me. I didn't know where it had come from, what had caused it. But something had flickered briefly in my mind, then faded away.

Benjamin's smile faltered. "We all missed you. Did you know that? Did you know that they tried very hard to trace you? But it was so strange. You and your mother disappeared into the city and that was the end of it. It was as if you'd been swallowed up."

I said, "I guess it seemed that way, Benjamin."

"The family is still there," he went on. "Still at Cornell House. Your aunt and uncle. Fernetta. My folks. It's just the same as it always was."

I knew the names, of course. Fernetta, my young first cousin. She had been eight years old the last time I saw her. Bernard, my father's brother. Sally, his wife. But they were all strangers to me now. I hadn't had a family for so long. I said, "I don't really remember much about them, Benjamin. After we left my mother never spoke of them. Children forget rather quickly."

"But why didn't you get in touch with us? Why didn't you ever visit us?"

I wondered about that myself. My mother had had a very small income. She had found it difficult to take care of us both all those years. She had been lonely, and bitter, and at the last, she had been terribly ill. Why had she turned her back on the only family she had?

"I never forgot you," Benjamin was saying. "I always hoped I'd find you again. And now that I have, I'm not going to let you go."

There would be love, Drago had told me. Love, and a tall dark man. Wealth and a long life and a happy future.

Benjamin's dark eyes smiled down at me. I was sure now that I recognized in him the tall dark, very quiet boy he had been at Cornell House. I imagined that I saw in him the lithe rider who had often accompanied my uncle and father in great gallops across the golden meadows beside the cliffs.

Benjamin's hands cupped my cheeks. A single finger traced out my dimples. He said, "Gaby, I mean it. I'm not going to let you go."

I said slowly, without planning the words, without the artifice to conceal what I already felt, "Benjamin, it's almost as if the gypsy's words are coming true, isn't it?"

"They will come true," he whispered. "I promise you that, Gaby."

I had come to the party alone, and in dread of the strangers I would meet. I left it with Benjamin, the strangers completely forgotten.

We had lit the candles at Jessie's insistence, and when I blew them out I made a silent wish. The wish came true.

Benjamin and I walked the miles back to my rooming house, and then sat together on the front steps, talking, until dawn.

"It's so odd," I said. "If I hadn't met Jessie, then I'd never have found you."

"It was meant to be," Benjamin answered. "Better believe in gypsies from now on."

"But how do you know Jessie?" I asked, suddenly curious. They had looked so good together. They had seemed so right. What if Jessie loved him, wanted him for herself?

"I've known Jessie several years, but just casually. I don't see her often. I rarely get into the city, you know. I don't much like it. I'll be going back in a couple of days, much to my relief. Anyhow, I was in on business, and walking down the street. I bumped into Jessie at a traffic light. She told me about the party, and invited me. She didn't mention your name, having no reason to suppose, I guess, that I'd recognize it. I didn't have anything better to do tonight, so I came. I was bored, thinking about leaving to tell you the truth, when you walked in the door. I knew you at once." He said teasingly, "And you might as well know that I was hurt that you didn't recognize me."

"But I did," I protested. "At least I think some part of me must have. Because I felt as if I might have seen you before. And I kept wishing you'd come and talk to me. I was so drawn to you, Benjamin." I stopped, my cheeks burning. I hadn't intended to admit that.

"Then you felt it, too," he said soberly.

"I kept wondering who you were, thinking that you seemed so familiar to me. As if I'd known you once. But I couldn't quite. . . ."

"Your mother really must have done a brainwashing job on you."

"Oh, no. She just never mentioned. . . ."

"Funny," he said. "Sally and Bernard so often spoke of you and her. It was always Rosalie this, and Gabriella that. They worried about you." He took my hand, held it tight. "But it's all in the past now. The family's completely forgiven her. And they had nothing to blame you for. You were only a child."

"I don't know what you're talking about," I said. "What do you mean? Completely forgiven my mother for what?"

"For running away the night of your father's funeral, of course. It was such a strange thing for her to do. It hurt them all terribly. That she should turn her back on them, take you away. But that was ten years ago, Gaby, no need to think of it now."

There was no use in thinking of it, and I didn't want to. I wanted to savor the miracle of our meeting. I said, "I kept wishing you'd come over— wondering why you didn't introduce yourself to me, wanting Jessie to do it, since you didn't seem to be willing to do it yourself. But you just hung back. . . ."

"I couldn't get over it," he explained. "I kept thinking that maybe I was mistaken. That maybe you had a twin, with your name as well as face. That maybe you weren't even real. I had to wait, to let it sink in." He leaned over me. "Gaby, I wonder if you really understand. It isn't just that I've found my cousin again." His deep voice became even deeper, a warm compelling whisper, "It's much more. I was telling you the truth when I said that I'd never forgotten you."

I didn't answer him. I couldn't.

He tipped my face up, kissed me lightly on the lips. "You think it's too fast, don't you? All right, I'll give you time, Gaby. I'll give you a chance to find out how you feel about me."

I knew how I felt about him. His smile, his touch, told me. But for just a moment I wondered why I remembered so little of him. I wondered why this seemed more a new meeting than a reunion.

I told myself that here was love, here my future. This was what Drago had promised me, if only I had the courage to meet it. I found the courage, brushing faint doubts away. I whispered, "I already know how I feel, Benjamin."

The next day I had lunch with Jessie. I wanted to treat her to a fancy meal in the Case Building coffee shop. But she insisted that we go to our usual cafeteria. When we had our salads and coffee, and were sitting at a corner table, she said, "You look as if you didn't have enough sleep, but it agrees with you."

"I had a wonderful time, Jessie."

"You enjoyed seeing your cousin again, didn't you?"

"More than that," I confessed.

"It's funny," she said, "how things work out. I've been hoping for the right man for so long, and you, just by a freak of fate, find him and know it without looking at all."

"The same thing will happen to you, too, Jessie, but just when you least expect it."

"As you never expected to see your cousin again?"

"Of course. I hadn't even thought of him in years. I think, if it hadn't been for you, Jess, I could have lived the rest of my life without thinking of him, too."

"And now?" she teased.

"You know the answer to that," I told her.

But my faint doubt returned when Benjamin met

me after work. He led me to his car. He drove to an overlook near the park, and stopped. He took my hand in his, slipped a big solitaire on my finger. "This is for you. It's an engagement ring. It used to belong to my mother."

It was beautiful. The symbol for which it stood was beautiful, too. But I hesitated, looking into his dark eyes.

"Don't you like it?" he demanded, "If you don't, I can. . . ."

"It's a lovely ring," I said slowly. "But. . . ."

"But what?"

I couldn't answer.

He touched the ring, turned it. "It fits just right. And it's perfect for you. I knew it would be."

"But Benjamin," I said slowly, "oughtn't we to wait a bit? Oughtn't we to make sure. . . ."

"Wait for what?" he asked. "I'm sure of how I feel about you. And I thought last night—this morning, rather, that you were sure of how you feel about me."

"Oh, yes, but. . . ."

"Then wait for what?"

"To get to know each other a little more. And then, what about your folks? Won't they think. . . ."

"I know you," he said. "I don't want to wait, Gaby."

"But you haven't seen me for ten years, Benjamin. You can't know me." I didn't add aloud that I hardly knew myself yet. But that was true, too.

His dark brows rose in quizzical arches. The warmth in his eyes seemed to cool. His long, narrow mouth thinned. "You don't trust me," he said slowly. "That's the truth of it isn't it? You don't trust me somehow. And that means that you don't love me."

"Marriage . . . Benjamin, it's something that's forever. Surely a few days. . . ."

"Then you shall have your few days," he grinned. "If you insist, I mean, then you may have them. All I want for you is to be happy, to feel as I do."

"I am happy," I said. "I do feel as you do."

"I hope so." He slid an arm around my shoulders.

"To have someone again. To love again. Not to be alone in the world," I whispered.

"You'll never be that," he promised me softly. "It must have been hard, Gaby, before. But that's all over now."

I lived in a bright dream. I had found Benjamin, and we would never be parted, I thought.

But two days later that bright dream nearly came to an end.

We were at dinner. The restaurant was small, dim. Benjamin looked at me across the red checked tablecloth and said, "Gaby, I'm going back to Cornell House tomorrow. I want you to come with me."

"Oh, but I can't," I protested. "I don't have any time off now. I'd lose my job, Benjamin."

He smiled faintly, "Gaby, you don't seem to understand. You won't need a job after we're married. I want you to quit work now."

"Why? Until we. . . ."

"It's time for you to come home, to meet the family again."

"I don't know," I told him, unable to explain to myself, to him, my hesitation. "Maybe we ought to wait just a little longer."

"My cautious darling," he smiled.

But later we stopped off at Jessie's for late coffee and cake.

Benjamin said, "Jessie, see if you can speak to this recalcitrant child."

"About what?" Jessie gave me a quick, three-cornered grin. I suddenly thought of a satisfied cat.

"There she sits," Benjamin said, "with her engagement ring on her hand, smiling so sweetly, but do you know she's perfectly willing for me to leave, which is what I'm going to do, and leave alone."

"Oh, I'm not willing," I said quickly, "and you know it. It's just that. . . ."

"She's not quite sure," Benjamin cut in. "Not of me. Not of herself. She wants to hang on to her job until she makes up her mind."

"You don't have to worry about Case, Gaby," Jessie told me. "I'll make sure that you can always have your job back. If you should want it. And the best way to make up your mind is to go with Benjamin, isn't it? Then you'll see him in his natural habitat. . . ."

"Which is also hers," Benjamin put in.

"And see your folks," Jessie went on.

"Who are more hers than mine," Benjamin added.

"And start living instead of existing," Jessie finished triumphantly.

Later, in the kitchen, she said quietly, "Gaby, are you out of your mind? Don't you know that any girl would give an arm or a leg to marry that marvelous man?"

I forced down a peculiar uneasiness. I said, "I do know it, Jessie. But it all . . . well, it just seems so fast."

"Isn't that how love always is?" Jessie asked.

3

THE DIRT ROAD wound higher and higher up the mountainside. At the crest there seemed nothing left but the soft haze of the blue sky.

Then we were over the crest. The sun glowed on the sloping meadows. A white house, big and low, with wide, sprawling wings, was agleam with sharp reflections. Neat terraces rimmed it, dropping down to the meadows, where scattered stands of pine stood like sentinels against the sky.

"Are you excited?" Benjamin asked me.

I clasped my hands, and the solitaire on my finger sparkled. I looked away from it quickly. What had been time dimmed recollections were suddenly clear and sharp memories. I knew this place. I knew the look and smell of it. It had once been home to me. But I was still dazed at the swiftness with which my life had been changed. One day I was a typist filling in multiple forms at Case Life and Casualty

and only a few days later, less than a week in actual
measure, I was engaged and on my way back to Cornell House, on my way to see a family I hadn't
known for ten years.

I looked sideways at Benjamin, met his smiling
gaze, and was instantly reassured. He loved me.
Everything would be all right.

"I suppose I am excited," I confessed.

"And a little scared, too?" he teased.

"Maybe a little," I agreed, determined to be honest,
though it might have been more politic to deny it.

"You oughtn't to be. You're with me. I'll make it
the way you want it to be. And besides, you're just
coming back to where you belong, Gaby."

I didn't doubt Benjamin then. I loved him, and I
had put my love and my life, too, in his hands. But
I knew, with a peculiar unease, that I had burned
all my bridges behind me. I had only a few dollars
in my purse, and no job to go back to. I had given
up my room, and no home remained for me to return to. It occurred to me then that my mother had
burned all her bridges when we left Cornell House,
and I now reversed the procedure. I found myself
wondering why we had not stayed on after my father
died. If we'd belonged, we would have, it seemed to
me. Life would have been easier, kinder for both of
us, I was sure. Then why had my mother been determined to leave the family, to leave Cornell House
behind? And if, as Benjamin had told me, the family
had searched for us, then why hadn't they found us?
We had only been in the city, some seventy miles
away. We had used our own name. Then I thought
of the unlisted number my mother had always
insisted on, saying that we could give to anyone we
wanted to hear from our telephone number. It

seemed a puny way to keep from being located, yet now I wondered if that had been what was in her mind. If the family had wanted to find us, I was sure that they could. But they hadn't. What had led to that so-deep separation?

Benjamin was asking insistently, "You do understand that this is your home, Gaby?"

"I suppose so," I agreed reluctantly.

His dark brows drew together in the quizzical frown that I loved. "But Gaby, you sound so unsure. Is there some reason, something I don't know about, that perhaps I ought to know about, that makes you uneasy about coming home?"

"No," I said hastily. "I can't think of any. It's just . . . well, to tell you the truth, Benjamin, I don't really feel that I'm coming home."

"You don't?"

"How can I? I hardly remember the place." But that wasn't quite true. As the car rolled down from the crest, along the steep inclines and the curves, everything around me grew more and more familiar. The pines, the eucalyptus, the golden meadows. . . .

"Surely you've begun to remember it all by now," he said.

"Yes," I agreed, But then I exclaimed, "There's something new, Benjamin. The pool. I don't remember the big pool."

"Yes. Johanna—my mother, that is, is fond of swimming." He went on, "No matter how you feel about it now, I want you to know how it really is." There was laughter in his voice, but a strong, firm undercurrent stressed his words and made them seem more serious than they sounded. "You do belong in Cornell House." He paused. Then, "Even more than I do."

"You?"

"Well, remember I'm a Haley. Not a Tysson."

"It's still one family," I protested.

"Of course. But there's something else you ought to know. The Haleys are the poor relations. We live in the cottage, surely you remember that much. We do try to give Bernard a hand with the responsibility of the property. But. . . ."

I wasn't listening. I had leaned forward. I could see the jagged cliffs that enclosed Cornell House grounds from the ocean below. The line of them seemed strange, irregular. I didn't know what was wrong.

Benjamin was saying "You do remember Cornell Cottage, don't you?" and pointing.

The image of it had been in my mind before it came into view. The square, white building, two stories high. The huge, plate glass windows that looked out on the meadows. Then I saw a tall man standing there—tall, and slim, and blond. My father. With him was Terrell Haley, dark, silky voiced. A shiver went over me. I didn't know why.

"Gaby?" Benjamin was asking.

"Yes," I breathed, "I remember it. It hasn't changed."

"No. Anyway not much. Bernard wouldn't care to spend too much on us, you know."

I raised my brows in a question.

He grinned, shrugged.

My eyes kept returning to the skyline of towering rocks. I wished I knew why it troubled me so.

Then Benjamin said, "I want you to understand how completely you belong here for a reason, Gaby."

Again I raised my brows in a question, but my heart began to beat very hard.

He grinned, "You look like a child halfway scared to death. And all I want to explain to you is the classical syndrome about possessive mothers and fathers and only sons."

"Oh," I said breathless with relief. "Oh, I see. Then you think your folks. . . ."

"No, darling, they won't run you out. How could they? No. What I mean is that if you feel a slight chill in the air, it's because they really want to keep me to themselves."

"I suppose I can't blame them." Then I twisted in my seat. "But Benjamin, didn't you tell them to expect me?"

"Not exactly."

I looked down at the solitaire he had given me. It was his mother's ring, he had said. If he hadn't told her about our engagement, then how had he happened to have it with him. It was a question that flickered briefly. I forgot it in the real impact of his words. "Benjamin! You mean they don't know I'm coming?"

"No, Gaby. And neither do Sally and Bernard."

"Oh, you shouldn't have done that," I wailed. "I don't think. . . ."

"Nonsense. I should and I did. I'm a grown man, twenty-eight years old. I marry when and whom I want to. And I have the right to bring my sweetheart home with me." He paused. Then added softly, "And since the sweetheart is you I have even more right."

"But what will they say?"

"Why, they'll freeze a bit, and then they'll wish us both good luck."

"They should have had warning, Benjamin."

"I don't see why. It wouldn't change anything." He grinned. "Of course there's Bernard and Sally.

They've rather had their eye on me for Fernetta, I guess. They'll be disappointed at the change I've made in their plans. But they'll be glad to have you back anyway."

I felt less than ever now like seeing my relatives. But as I looked around me it was like seeing a dream become reality. I sensed the familiar and the strange. I knew I had ridden along the same road before, studied the same scenery, yet I couldn't place it all in time.

"It's beautiful, isn't is?" Benjamin asked.

"Oh yes," I breathed.

"Worth anything to keep," he went on. And then, "I'll never never understand how your mother could bear to leave here."

I didn't answer him. I was finding it harder and harder to understand that myself. What I had once taken so for granted that I never even thought of it, was now a matter for pyramiding questions.

"She must have had her reasons, of course."

"She never spoke of them," I said.

"Never told you what happened?" he asked.

"No."

"Oh, she must have, Gaby. She surely explained. If there was an explanation."

"There might not have been. If there was, she didn't bother to inform me of it. She just decided to leave, and decided when, and. . . ."

Benjamin mused, "The night your father was buried."

The car was moving so slowly now it seemed to drift along the dirt road. Behind it there rose a gentle curtain of golden dust.

"It was odd," he went on. "We none of us expected it. She simply disappeared. We knew that

she hated us, but no one thought that she could carry
it so far."

"Hated you?" I asked. "Why should she hate the
family, Benjamin?"

He shrugged his wide shoulders. "Who knows?
Some times when women feel that they haven't had
their husbands' full attention they tend to blame
whomever they can."

I gave him a cool steady look. "My father and
mother were deeply in love, Benjamin. Whatever
else I've forgotten or never knew, I do remember
that. And I remember how my mother was afterwards."

I remembered her weeping, the anguished denial
in her face. I remembered how she was in the years
after.

Benjamin touched my arm gently. "Listen, Gaby,
you mustn't think I meant anything derogatory by
that. I was only half guessing what it could have
been. Not even that really. Just speculating. I was
a kid myself in those days. I didn't know what was
going on any more than you did."

The words, the gentle tone, were mollifying. I
leaned back, forgetting my sudden defensiveness.

Benjamin eased the car around the last curve, and
guided the car into a parking area behind the house.

"Ready?" he asked.

I nodded, but my heart began again to beat very
quickly. I might have once known these people I was
about to meet, but now they were strangers. They
would weigh me, and wonder. They would look at
Benjamin, and then at me, and they would cover
bewilderment with a hypocritical courtesy.

Benjamin said, "Gaby, stop it. You're going to
be happy here. Just remember that. No matter what

happens. Remember that I love you, and I'm going to make you happy here."

He hugged me to him briefly, then let me go, and we got out of the car together. He led the way along a narrow terrace path beneath the stacked shrubberies, around to the front of the house.

There he paused again. He grinned, bent to kiss me. I clung to him briefly.

At that moment, the big front door flew open. It slammed back so hard that the huge brass knocker on it cracked twice. In the sweet still air the sound was like two pistols echoing across the meadows.

I let Benjamin go, my cheeks burning.

He turned leisurely, smiling his tilted smile.

A high backed wheelchair rolled to the edge of the terrace steps and stopped with a jerk.

"Benjamin! It's about time you came home. What on earth have you been doing? Where have you been? We've all been three-quarters out of our minds with worry about you."

The voice was shrill, petulant, demanding. The girl from whose lips it issued had a great sheaf of raven black hair and wide open blue eyes. Her mouth was thin, and fell naturally into a pout.

I knew her instantly and was shaken by the recognition.

She was Fernetta Tysson, Sally and Bernard's daughter. She was two years younger than I was, and the last time I had seen her she had been small, plump, and laughing. I remembered her as part lovable pest, who trailed me wherever I went, and part doll with which I could play.

I couldn't tell if she knew me.

Benjamin led me to her. "I've brought Gaby home

to you, Fernetta. Now do you understand where I've been this last week?"

Fernetta's wide blue eyes stared at me emptily. A meaningless smile tipped her pouting lips. She said, in a flat voice, with neither welcome nor joy, "Gaby. Gabriella. After all this time. . . ."

"You do remember each other?" Benjamin asked, looking at me.

I tried to shake the chill that touched me. The chill at finding her in a wheelchair. The chill at her reception of me. I forced a smile, cried, "Fernetta, it's been years and years, but you look almost the same."

"Almost," Fernetta said emptily.

Her blue eyes dropped to regard the tan jeans she wore. They revealed too-thin, wasted legs.

I thought of a little girl, small, dark haired, perhaps seven or eight. A girl who had run and danced and jumped from terrace to terrace. She hadn't spent her days in a wheelchair, useless legs dangling in tan trousers, thin fingers curling and uncurling on her knees.

My throat felt tight with sympathy. Fernetta had earned the right to be petulant, even to be—suspicious was the word I thought of. That was what I felt.

Her blue eyes swept me in an all encompassing glance. She made my feelings into words. "You really are Gabriella Tysson?"

"Not as I am now. But as I was then."

"Of course," I said gently, "And I remember you very well, Fernetta."

There was nothing I could say in answer to that.

After a moment, she went on. "We played together." The words came out in an unwilling rush. "We had a good time. It was so different then. It was before all the bad things began to happen." The words stopped. She spun the wheelchair away from the edge of the steps. She said, as she disappeared around the corner of the house, "You shouldn't have come back, Gaby."

I blinked, glanced at Benjamin. I hadn't expected her to express her displeasure so overtly. I wondered why she was so displeased.

He grinned, shook his head. "You mustn't take Fernetta too literally, Gaby. She's very changed by the accident, you know. It's made her bitter, and I can't say I blame her. Being confined to a wheelchair. . . ."

"What happened to her?" I asked.

But Benjamin didn't answer me. He said, "Let's go find the others," and went ahead of me into a long dim hallway.

Gold framed portraits hung on the white walls. Tyssons, I knew, male and female, who had lived in Cornell House generations before. The stairway was broad and high, leading to the second floor, and covered with a deep pile green carpet.

Benjamin flung back a pair of sliding doors.

We stood on the threshold together.

The room was big, its size and brightness emphasized by white walls on which a grouping of paintings seemed to stand out. They were the horses that my father had loved, bred and raised here at Cornell House.

A rug of gold seemed woven of sunlight.

The furniture was pale fruitwood, and aglow from years of careful waxing.

This was called the morning room.

My mother had read to me here. She and my father

had had coffee together at the table under the window.

But now four people sat at that table. With the bright sun streaming through they seemed like still silhouettes only.

Obviously we had interrupted them at cards. They turned their heads slowly. Four faces studied me blankly.

Benjamin said, "I've brought Gaby Tysson home with me."

The room was utterly still.

There wasn't a sound, a movement.

It was as if all of us had stopped breathing.

Then Benjamin said, "I know that you're very surprised. Shocked, even, that after all this time I was able to find her. But it was easier than you'd think. I didn't even have to look. A friend of mine works in the same place that Gaby did. We met at a party. . . ."

The peculiar silence continued.

I heard my pulses beat in my ears.

I looked into the blank faces.

Benjamin laughed. "I have another surprise. Gaby's going to marry me in a few days."

Where there had been silence before there was now a vast, echoing emptiness. Within it, I felt myself cringe. I wished suddenly that I hadn't allowed Benjamin to persuade me to give up my job and come here, to this place that I barely remembered, to see people whom I hardly knew. It wasn't like me to act in such an incautious fashion. I supposed I had let myself be convinced because I wanted so much to be. Because I couldn't face the possibility of losing Benjamin—love—just when I'd found him. But now under the impact of such open but wordless disapproval I wanted to be back in the city, with Jessie to talk to, my job to do, my small room to hide in.

"Forgive me if I perform unnecessary introductions," Benjamin was saying. "But Gaby remembers very little of any of us. You see Rosalie just never spoke of Cornell House, or of us." He moved his sleek, dark head. "Your Aunt Sally Tysson, Gaby."

The slat thin, gray haired woman stared at me with wide open, empty blue eyes just like Fernetta's. Then suddenly she smiled, got to her feet.

I knew her then. I remembered her. I was startled that ten years could have changed her from the bright faced young woman that I had known.

She came across the room, moving slowly, as if she had barely enough strength to walk. She looked down at me, then took me by the hand. She led me to the window, and peered down into my face. I squinted into the too-bright sunlight.

"Gaby," she said. "Gabriella. It *is* you, isn't it?" She turned, her blues eyes focusing on the table. "Yes, Bernard. It's Gaby all right."

My uncle deliberately laid down his cards. He folded plump hands and peered at me through narrowed brown eyes. The scar on his forehead glowed red.

Oddly, it was then that I remembered having seen him—forehead bandaged, nose and chin bandaged. I remembered that Sally had been weeping, and that my father had been angry. But that was all I remembered. It hadn't mattered then.

Bernard said, "Welcome back to Cornell House, Gabriella."

Benjamin didn't allow the heavy silence to return.

He picked up quickly. "My parents, Gaby. Johanna and Terrell. Perhaps you remember them?"

Johanna was tall, blonde, beautiful. She had changed not a bit since I was little, if I could go by the very faint recollection I had of her.

"You were a very pretty child indeed," she said finally. "You've grown up to be a pretty girl."

"We're always happy to welcome pretty girls into our family," Terrell said silkily. He was an older version of Benjamin. His hair was dark, swept across his forehead in a single wave, but the temples were touched with silver. He was slim, tall, but just beginning now to thicken. His face was lean, his eyes dark, set in a map of lines.

Benjamin said, "It was lucky, Mother, that I had the solitaire with me to get it repaired. It was the day I retrieved it from the jewelers that I met Gaby. I knew right away I'd better just hang on to it."

"It's a beautiful ring," I told Johanna. "Are you sure you want me to have it?"

"Of course," Johanna said, but her voice was cool. She seemed to notice that herself. She smiled, then went on, "Benjamin's always known it was to go to his fiancée."

"How old are you, Gabriella?" Bernard asked.

"Just about twenty-one," I told him. "It was at a slightly premature twenty-first birthday party that I met Benjamin."

"When will it be your real birthday?" Terrell asked.

"In three weeks," Benjamin answered, speaking for me.

There were quick, running footsteps in the hall.

The double doors clattered as they were thrown back.

I turned, expectant without knowing why.

A small, plump woman swept into the room as if spun along on a whirlwind. A full dark skirt billowed around her calves. A loose white blouse flopped around her round shoulders. Her gray-white hair was wisped into a flyaway bun on her wrinkled neck. Her rimless glasses sat askew on her short, upturned nose.

I knew her instantly. The others had been vague memories only, and they seemed different now. But Helen Beck was the same. She was exactly the same as she had been when I was ten years old and had sat in the kitchen and watched her bake gingerbread men while Fernetta played jacks on the floor. Helen was the same as when she had bandaged my ripped knees when I fell off the terrace. She was the same as she had been the night she kissed me and my mother goodbye.

Now she cried, "Gaby, oh, Gaby, is it you? Is it really you? Have you truly come back at last?"

Here were arms to hold me, a shoulder to cling to. I went to her in a quick rush. I hugged her and held her.

"Helen," I whispered, "I'm so glad to see you. It's been years and years, but. . . ."

"You remember me then, love? You haven't forgotten?"

"Of course not." I felt my smile grow and grow, until it felt as if it would split my face. "Now I know that I'm home, Helen."

"Yes, love, you are, you are, and don't ever forget it." She settled her glasses on her upturned nose. "And Rosalie? How's our lovely Rosalie? And where is she, and. . . ."

Benjamin cut in, "Oh, Helen, can't you use some tact? Gaby's mother is dead."

Helen's round face seemed to shrink. The joyful smile went out of her eyes. She muttered, "I'm sorry, Gaby." She paused, swallowed. "I should have thought . . . but she was so young still . . . it just never . . . oh, love, forgive me if I hurt you."

"You didn't, Helen. You couldn't." I could easily reassure her. Helen hadn't hurt me, nor intended to. I had been remembering my mother, her death, ever since I returned to Cornell House.

Benjamin said, "You haven't asked why Gaby's here, Helen. You don't know the news."

She looked at him, then at me. She waited.

He said, "We're going to be married in a few days' time."

Helen gasped, "But Gaby, you can't, you can't!"

Benjamin's grin hardened on his lips. His dark brows flattened out.

But before he could speak, Johanna said from her place at the table, "Why, really, Helen, you do forget yourself. I realize that you consider yourself a member of the family. But actually you're just a servant here. I hope you'll try to remember that in the future."

Rich color flooded Helen's face, then faded, leaving her pale. She stammered, "Oh, I beg your pardon, I was just so . . . so stunned. You understand, don't you? It's just. . . ." Helen's eyes sought mine. "You're so young, Gaby. You're not yet twenty-one, are you? And you can't have known Benjamin long enough . . . if you had, we'd have heard."

"We're in love," I told her. "And look. . . ." I held out the solitaire for her to see. "Benjamin's given me his mother's ring."

Her lips twisted as if to answer.

But Bernard spoke from across the room. "We understand, Helen. We're all just as surprised, just as happy as you are."

I knew that Benjamin and I had shocked them. I wished now, more than ever before, that he had let them know ahead of time. They had been too shocked, I thought. But happy? I wondered if they were really happy.

4

I WAS UNPACKING. I worked quicky, putting away
the stocking and lingerie, the blouses, and scarves.
I hung up my dresses and skirts and pants suits.
I had so much to think about. It required effort to
force my concentration on the homely tasks. There
were impressions to sort out, and study, to attempt
finally to understand. To be busy, moving quickly
from the bed on which my open suitcase lay, to the
wide, white painted dresser across the pale blue
room, was an evasion. I decided that I would allow
myself that for a little while. The sooner I was
settled, the more comfortable I would feel.

But I wondered if being settled would really make
that much difference.

I had come to Cornell House in trepidation, and
nothing in the welcome I had received had helped
to ease it. More than ever now, I felt alone.

Plainly neither Johanna nor Terrell were anxious

53

to have me as Benjamin's wife. As he had warned me, they must be possessive parents, hungering to keep their only son. I knew it wouldn't be easy to win them. I wasn't sure that I could. My Aunt Sally had seemed oddly suspicious, as if Benjamin might somehow or other have brought back with him an impostor, for what purpose I couldn't imagine. Then, when she decided I was the *real* Gabriella Tysson, she seemed more thoughtful than joyful. My Uncle Bernard's scar had glowed red, and he had peered at me, and I hadn't been able to tell what he was thinking.

Only Helen had been truly happy to see me, and then even she, sweet, good Helen, had seemed more frightened than glad to hear that I was to marry Benjamin.

My uneasiness, so faint before that I could ignore it, had become a deep running current. It was as if the fragile leaves of my happiness and hope for the future had begun to grow seared at their tips. I tried hard to thrust the thought away from me, but I wished I had Jessie to talk to. She was so cool, so knowing. She might understand. She might be able to reassure me.

I closed the last drawer, and went to the wide open window. I stood there, looking down at the golden meadows. Horses grazed there, many more than I had remembered from childhood. A big, black stallion, a huge palomino, two roans. My gaze returned to the stallion. A shiver went over me. He reminded me of Satan's Son, my father's horse. The one from which he had fallen to his death. I forced my gaze away from him to the cliff wall. Once again I was troubled by the sight of ocean and sky through a great raw-looking gap. I was about to turn away when I heard from below the sound of soft voices.

Soft, yes, almost strained whispers. But I could hear them clearly.

Sally was saying, "It *is* Gaby. I'm sure."

"That's who she says she is. We don't know that. We can't be sure," Uncle Bernard protested thickly. "And you know Benjamin . . . he'd do anything. . . ."

"She's Denby's daughter," Sally insisted. "I believe Benjamin that far."

"I wash my hands of it: That's all," Bernard said. "I just wash my hands of it."

"Bernard, no, you . . ."

"Yes," he retorted.

"He takes too much on himself, Bernard."

"Let Johanna and Terrell worry about it. I won't. I can't. There's nothing I can do, I tell you."

"There's Joshua Horn. The lawyers. When they hear. . . ."

"Leave me alone," Bernard said hoarsely. "I tell you, you must leave me alone."

The voices stopped abruptly. But the sound of them echoed in my ears. Sally had sounded dazed, frightened. But Bernard had seemed . . . the only word I could think of was terrified. Why should he be terrified of me? What could I do to harm him?

I turned away from the window, wishing I hadn't overheard that conversation. It had given me more to think about. More I didn't want. I wished I was with Benjamin, snuggled in his arms, listening to him tell me about the future we would share.

But the name I heard, Joshua Horn, stuck in my thoughts. It was several minutes before I could actually attach it to a face, a man. He had been a friend of my father's—small, quick, elderly. They had often played chess together. Once I had identified him, I remembered what Sally had said about lawyers. What possible interest could they have in me?

I was glad for the interruption of a knock at the door. "Come in," I called, hoping it would be Benjamin.

But when the door opened, Fernetta sat there in her wheelchair. Her wide blue eyes studied me up and down. "Are you finishing unpacking?"

"Yes, I am."

We had been friends once, I thought. I hoped we could be friends again. But I sensed a wall of reserve between us. She was no longer the small, dancing girl who had followed me eagerly about.

She said, "It didn't take you very long, Gaby."

"I don't have all that much."

Her blue eyes peered past me into the room. "This is the room you had when you were little, isn't it?"

"Yes. It is, I think. At least that one was blue, and this one is, and I think I remember the view of the cliffs. But. . . ." I turned, gave her a puzzled look. "Fernetta, the view looks different. It keeps bothering me."

She smiled suddenly. "It *is* different, Gaby. Lovers Leap is gone."

I gave the cliff line a quick look, and suddenly saw in my mind the great, towering rock that had once filled the raw, open place that looked down into the ocean so far below. Yes, oh, yes, of course. That's what had bothered me. Lovers Leap, one of our most obvious landmarks, was gone.

"But what happened?" I asked.

"The earthquake in February. It broke away and slid off. It was terrible, Gaby. I was still in bed. The house shook and swayed, and some of the windows broke, and I thought the world was coming to an end when that part of the cliff let go."

"It was the same in the city. I had just gotten up to see if my mother wanted anything. And all the pictures fell off the walls."

"Your mother," Fernetta said softly, "I remember her so well, Gaby. She was a lovely woman, beautiful to look at, to know, too. She and your father. . . ." Fernetta's wide open blue eyes met mine, then skidded away to stare at the window. "It was so different after they were gone."

"Different?"

"Can't you see it? Feel it?"

"I don't remember that much, Fernetta."

"It must have been hard on you and Aunt Rosalie. You must have been poor. But you were free, Gaby." Fernetta's thin fingers worked convulsively at the arms of the wheelchair. "Yes," she whispered, "you were free."

"Weren't you? Aren't you?"

But she ignored my questions. She studied the room, said, "Of course the furniture's new, the rug. Johanna loves to redecorate. My father lets her do what she wants to. So there have been quite a few changes."

"The pool," I said.

"Johanna's a great swimmer," Fernetta said dryly. "Though she insisted it was the greatest therapy in the world for me."

"And there are no dogs," I said. "I remember that we always used to have a lot of dogs."

"Terrell insists that they harassed the horses." Fernetta took a deep, obvious breath. She went on, "But you can have them if you want, Gaby. You can have anything you want."

"But if Terrell doesn't. . . ."

Fernetta spun her wheelchair around. "I was on my way to Cornell Cottage. Do you want to come with me?"

"If you like," I answered. I gave myself a quick look in the mirror. My blonde curls were as tousled as always. I brushed them back, knowing that brief discipline would do no good, and dabbed at my nose with powder. Then, Fernetta led the way to the back of the hall. There, under the rising staircase, I found one more thing that had been added to Cornell House in my absence. A small elevator.

"It was put in for me after I had my accident," Fernetta said.

Again I wondered how she had been injured. It seemed unkind to ask so I didn't. I only hoped that Fernetta would somehow explain. But Fernetta didn't.

She thrust back the small, grilled doorway, rolled herself inside. I followed. The mesh case dropped slowly in response to Fernetta's touch at the controls.

On the first floor I opened the grill again.

Fernetta rolled herself through.

We were at the rear of the long hall that led to the front door. The broad staircase was above us.

Fernetta said, "There's a ramp out back. It's a lot easier for me that way."

I followed her out of the house and down the path through the lower terraces. She handled the wheelchair adeptly, and I had to hold my hands at my sides to keep from offering to help her, knowing with certainty that she wouldn't want me to.

At the west terrace, she stopped.

From there I could see the white square outlines

of the cottage, shadowing the stables and corral, and behind it the rising cliff wall. I felt a shiver touch me. I didn't like that place. I didn't know why. Benjamin had always lived there, I reminded myself, and lived there still. Yet, strangely, I couldn't really remember him sitting on those front steps. I had a faint impression that I had seen him at the corral, but nothing more than that.

Fernetta asked, "Gaby, are you really going to stay here then?"

"Yes. I think so. For a while at least."

"And you're really going to marry Benjamin?"

I looked down at the gleaming solitaire on my finger. I was sorry for her. There had been a wistful note in her voice, a sad one. Finally I had to answer her. I said, "Yes, Fernetta, we're in love. I'm going to marry Benjamin."

"Do you think you should?"

"I don't understand."

She said wryly, "I guess you're wondering what gives me the right to question you."

"I don't mind, Fernetta. It's just that . . . well, I don't understand. Everyone seems so . . . so against me. And I don't know why. I don't. . . ."

"It's a mistake," Fernetta said in a tense whisper. "That's why they feel that way."

"But why?"

Fernetta's blue eyes peered into my face for a long time, then swerved away to the sloping meadows. "It is, that's all. Take my word for it. I can't tell you more than that. But I know, we all know. Oh, Gaby, if only you hadn't come back."

She was suddenly the small girl I remembered. I wanted to hug and reassure her. But then the full

impact of her words struck me. She was sorry I'd
returned. We weren't, and couldn't be, friends.

I demanded, "Fernetta, tell me the truth. Why
don't you want me here?"

"It's not that I don't want you!" she whispered.
There was a faint sheen of perspiration on her upper lip. Her thin hands convulsively gripped the
wheelchair arms. At last she went on, "It's just that
. . . well, you haven't known Benjamin very long,
have you? Not since you've been grown up."

I asked gently, "Fernetta, did your parents tell you
to speak to me about this?"

She jerked her head up, and the black, glossy
hair whipped around her thin face. "My parents
can't talk me into anything." She whipped the
wheelchair around, sent it rolling down the path.

I followed her to Cornell Cottage.

Benjamin came out to meet us. He had changed
to a white silk shirt and sleek fitted chinos. His dark
hair was brushed smoothly across his forehead. I
was so glad to see him that I wanted to fling myself
into his arms. Only Fernetta's presence held me
back.

He grinned his tilted grin, asked, "All settled and
at home?"

Fernetta cut in, "She's unpacked. If that's what
you mean. She says she'll stay here. And I guess
she'll tell you that I tried to run her off so I might
as well tell you that myself first."

There was defiance in her voice, but her eyes regarded Benjamin anxiously. My heart gave a wrench
of sympathy for her.

He laughed, said, "Fernetta, darling, you're in-
corrigible." And to me, "Fernetta has long considered me her private property."

It was plainly supposed to be a cousinly joke. But I remembered that Benjamin had told me that Bernard and Sally had once hoped that Benjamin and Fernetta would become interested in each other. Now I knew that he had not become interested in Fernetta, but she had in him. She was in love with him. It was in her eyes, her lips. It was in the way her frail body inclined in her wheelchair toward him. Now I knew why she was sorry I had returned, why she insisted that I oughtn't to marry Benjamin. And her reasons must be her parents' reasons, too. But Helen . . . what of dear Helen, whom I had always trusted and loved? *You can't, you can't,* she had cried. Then I knew the answer to that. She had, over the years, given her affection, her pity, too, to Fernetta. Didn't she, the rest of them, understand that they couldn't make Benjamin want Fernetta rather than me?

Now Fernetta turned her wheelchair. She rolled up the path slowly and laboriously.

Benjamin's dark eyes followed her. "Poor girl. It's been hard on her."

"Of course," I agreed. I tried to imagine what it would be like to be crippled like that, to be unable to walk, dance, to look forward to love. A shiver went over me. I saw Fernetta stop on the lower terrace, resting, I supposed. Her face, revealed in a ray of sunlight, was staring down, twisted with some emotion I couldn't identify? Was it jealousy? Or was it fear?

Benjamin took my arm. "Let's have a walk. I want to show you around. I want you to feel settled right away. And. . . ." He paused. Then, "Mostly I guess I'm curious to see how much you actually remember."

"Just a little," I said indifferently. That seemed so unimportant to me. Why should Benjamin care? "Some of the house. My room." I looked along the sloping meadows, the stands of pine, the corral and stables, and the cottage. "It's familiar. All this. But in a blurred way."

He tucked my hand under his arm, drew me with him toward the jagged cliffs.

I looked at the raw slash of color that divided them into two separate walls of lichen covered granite.

"Lovers Leap is gone."

"The earthquake," Benjamin said.

"Fernetta was telling me. It was terrifying, wasn't it?"

"For a few moments only."

We had reached the cliffs by then, the open place where Lovers Leap had been.

I followed him reluctantly onto the tilted granite to the very edge. There, for the first time since my return, I had a clear view of the ocean far below, of the white, rock strewn beach.

Where we stood the sun was warm and sweet and golden, but the shore itself lay in shadow.

"It looks lonely," I whispered.

"It is. And that's how we like it, Gaby. No trespassing here. No campers, or weekenders, to be concerned with. No intrusions, and no trash, no fires to worry about."

White spume fluttered like banners against the base of the cliff as waves rolled in. Gulls swooped and spun and screamed on the quick air currents. Then, very slowly, the shadowed darkness of the beach below seemed to reach up, enveloping us where we stood. The sun was gone behind a thick bank of clouds.

I shuddered and turned away.

Benjamin said, "What's left to Lovers Leap is still down there. That big flat rock with the split shaped like an arrow."

But I refused to look back. I edged away, and he followed me.

"Benjamin," I asked now, "tell me what happened to Fernetta."

For the second time, I noticed, he evaded me. He shrugged, said, "Ancient history, Gaby. Nothing to do with you. You mustn't let the poor child's moods infect you." Then, before I could protest, he asked, "Do you still like to ride?"

"I haven't for years, you know. Not since we left here."

"It's like bicycling," he assured me. "You never forget it once you've learned."

"I suppose," I agreed absently. I was thinking of my parents. My father had been an avid horseman, my mother an unwilling horsewoman. He had died on Satan's Son, and she had wept. I wasn't sure that I wanted to try riding again.

But Benjamin said, "It's one of our few entertainments, practically our reason for existence here, Gaby."

"I suppose it is."

He stopped. His arms came around me. "You sound so woebegone. Please don't feel that way. I want you to be happy."

I smiled at him. "I am, Benjamin. It's just that. . . ." I looked up into his intent dark eyes, seeing the quizzical arch in his brows. "It's just that you don't realize how unused to all this I am. In the city, at home, I'd have been at work for hours. I'd have my job to do. . . ."

"This is your home, Gaby," he said insistently.

"You know what I mean. I guess I don't quite know what to do with myself without my little routine."

I wanted to believe that, and in a way, I thought it to be true. But there was something else. Something I didn't want to mention. I had returned to Cornell House dreading my meeting with the family I had once known but knew no longer. I had braced myself to be exposed to strangers. And I knew I was unwelcome. That was what really troubled me. I didn't want to tell Benjamin that, however.

Benjamin was laughing, "But, darling," he said, sounding very much as he had when he spoke to Fernetta earlier, "You'll get used to it soon enough. I thought it was every working girl's dream to lie in bed late, to switch off the alarm clock and go back to sleep. I thought leisure was what she'd desire above everything else."

"When you don't have it, maybe it seems more important than it is," I told him. "But remember, Benjamin, I've had my chores to do, my responsibilities, my interests, for ten years. All that is part of what I am. Maybe I can't change into someone else."

"I don't want you to," he said. "I want you to stay you, Gaby."

But I was sorry now that I had burned all my bridges behind me. Sorry I had let Benjamin's insistence, and Jessie's encouragement, lead me to act against my own nature. I should have stayed where I was. Benjamin could have come in to visit me. After a brief engagement, we could have been married.

"You're so quiet," he said. "Tell me what you're thinking."

I didn't want to put it into words. I had chosen. It was done. I was here.

He said softly, "You mustn't pay any attention to the rest of them, Gaby. I'm the one that's important to you. I'm the one that loves you. I'm the one that counts."

I melted against him. Those were the words I needed, the feelings I had to hear expressed, the reassurance that supported me. "I know, Benjamin. But they don't want me here. And I feel it."

He held me close. "Never mind them, Gaby. Just think of me. Remember me. And everything will be all right."

The sun rimmed the black cliffs and touched the terrace with fading carmine. Blue twilight still hung over the meadows.

We were all on the flower scented and umbrella decorated terrace together.

Benjamin had just served a round of before dinner drinks, and now he sat on the white wrought iron bench beside me.

I sipped gingerale in the thick silence, feeling as if I were the center of a ring of censuring eyes.

At last Sally stirred, said thickly, "I suppose you do resemble Denby somewhat, Gabriella."

I smiled faintly, wondering if she had begun drinking earlier than the rest of us. I said, "Perhaps I do, just a little."

"But you look much more like Rosalie," Sally went on, as if in accusation.

"I see no resemblance to either of them," Bernard put in heavily, his jowls pink and full and quivering, and the scar on his forehead suddenly red. "If there's any Tysson in this child it surely doesn't show."

Fernetta smiled thinly, turned to me. "Don't listen to them. They always think out loud. Wishful thinking out loud, I should say."

Terrell stretched out his long legs, said silkily, "And you were always an impertinent child."

Fernetta ignored him. Her blue eyes sought mine. She said earnestly, "Gaby, you know what they say, don't you? Never trust anybody over thirty. Well, you think about it and remember it."

Sally cut in quickly. "That will do, Fernetta," and went on to Benjamin, "Perhaps there's time for one more round?"

He rose, went into the house.

Terrell smiled at me, his lean face so like Benjamin's that it hurt me a little. I didn't know why. He said quietly, "I think I should explain Fernetta's rather unkind remark, which was, of course, directed at me." He spoke as if she were invisible, unfeeling. He said, "She blames me for her fate, you see. We were steeplechasing. She fell. So she blames me." He shrugged. "It's irrational, but a fact. I can hardly blame her though."

"So kind of you to understand," Fernetta jeered.

Benjamin returned carrying a loaded tray. As he passed the glasses around, he said to the company at large, "Perhaps this will help the bunch of you remember your manners. After all, we do have a guest in our midst."

"But Gaby's family," Johanna said. "She's a Tysson. That makes her family, doesn't it?"

5

It was still early, but I made my excuses and retreated to my room shortly after dinner.

Benjamin had protested that he wanted to take me for a moonlight ride along the cliffs. But I told him I would prefer to try my long lost skill by day and sun. Then he had suggested that we take a drive in the hills. But I had said I was too tired.

Now I was settled beside the window in an antique rocker, a book I had borrowed from the morning room shelves below lying unread on my lap.

It was such a relief to be alone, to try to collect my scattered impressions, to try to fit them to my small store of meager memories.

The blue room, half familiar, half strange, seemed to whisper to me. I thought of the night my mother had awakened me from an exhausted sleep. I remember my mother's cold hands, as they hurried me into my clothes, and Helen's anxious whispers. I recalled clearly the quick, tiptoeing departure, the fog against the windshield as the car crept down the road.

Now, suddenly, there were twin headlights on that same road.

I watched them creep along the curves, rising, dipping. I watched them splash the junipers and pines and sliver the eucalyptus.

I hadn't heard a car drive away. So no one was returning. I wondered who could be arriving. It was already plain to me that there was little entertaining, if any, done at Cornell House. I was surprised that no one had mentioned that guests were expected.

Soon I heard the slam of a car door. There was a moment or two of silence, then I heard exclamations.

Fernetta cried, "William! Oh, William, where did you drop from? It's been ages and ages since we saw you. I didn't know you were coming."

There was a false note in her voice, a certain frantic shrillness. I wondered if she was outside the house alone.

I leaned closer to the window, peered down.

Fernetta was just below, on the terrace. White spotlights spilled a glow around her, and on the man who stood with her.

I caught a glimpse of a square face, wide shoulders. William, Fernetta had called him. I wondered who he was.

"I've been busy," he was saying. "My time isn't exactly my own, you know. But I'm here now."

He had a slow, quiet voice. The words came out as if each one had been carefully considered.

Fernetta said, "What a fuss there's been. Can you imagine what Benjamin's gone and done?"

William laughed. "I think I'm afraid to try. So suppose you tell me."

"He was in the city for a few days. I don't know why he went. You know how he hates to leave this place. Anyhow, he did go. And he met Gaby. Gaby Tysson. You remember who she is, don't you, William? My first cousin. Denby Tysson's little girl. But now she's all grown up, of course. Benjamin ran into her by accident, and it was love at first sight, and he's brought her back here with him."

William didn't answer for a moment. Then he said, "That's strange, isn't it? After all those years. . . ."

"She and her mother, Aunt Rosalie, lived in the city all this time, she says. I guess the family didn't look for them quite hard enough."

"I guess not," William agreed.

The family didn't look for them quite hard enough.

Those words struck me as exceedingly odd.

Benjamin had once said something about the family's having searched for my mother and me. Still I couldn't, now, quite remember what his words had actually been.

But hearing the conversation below, I suddenly realized that we had slipped away from Cornell House and virtually gone into hiding. Was that what was implied? Mother had been frightened. It hadn't been the grief of my father's sudden death that had driven her away. It had been fear. Yet it didn't seem to me that we had actually been in hiding. We hadn't changed our names, for instance. If anyone had really looked hard for us, we should have been easy enough to locate. And here was William implying that no one had looked very hard.

A ripple of my mother's old fear touched me now. There was too much that I didn't understand.

"Come in," Fernetta was saying. "Just wait until the rest of them see you."

The false, frantic note was still in her voice. I found it hard to believe in what she was saying.

William laughed, "I don't expect the fatted calf to welcome me, Fernetta."

The voices faded away. A heavy door slammed.

I rose from the rocker, put my book aside.

Even more now I wondered who William was. I hadn't heard of him, yet he had plainly recognized my name.

I suppose I would find out in the morning, if he was still there.

I was about to turn down the bedspread when Helen tapped at my door, called to me.

I let her in. Her gray-white hair was wisped around her face. Her glasses were askew on her nose. She breathed as if she had been running.

"Are you comfortable, love?"

I invited her in with a gesture.

She scurried to the rockingchair and sank into it with a sigh. She folded her hands in her lap, blue eyes fixed on my face. "Well, love, *are* you comfortable?"

"Yes. I'm all settled, Helen."

Her fingers plucked her black skirt. She said, "It's different."

I nodded. "But pleasant." I thought she meant the furniture, the rugs and drapes throughout the house.

She seemed to understand my confusion. "I don't mean that." She flapped her hands. "That's just things. I mean . . . I mean . . . well, the atmosphere. You find it pleasant?"

"I guess so." I paused. Then, "But I haven't been here very long, Helen."

She ignored that. She asked. "How was it for you, Gaby?"

"What do you mean?"

"Your life. After you and your mother went away from here."

I shrugged. "Why, I don't know how to describe it. We were together. We had each other. We were a family. I took it for granted, Helen."

"It must have been a struggle though. Your mother must have found it terribly hard. She had been used to so much, you know. Your father had always provided the best. And then, so suddenly, to. . . ." Helen stopped herself. Her pale lips folded together.

I said, "I guess it was hard. But I don't know. We just managed. She had the small income, of course."

"That one from her own folks." Helen nodded. "And nothing else."

I shook my head.

"And after she died?"

"The income stopped. But I'm grown now, Helen. I had taken a business course. When I was alone, I got myself a job. We had planned it out before hand, you know. My mother insisted."

"She was always a brave one," Helen sighed. "And it wasn't what your father had planned for you, Gaby."

I didn't know what to say. I didn't answer her.

"And you met Benjamin through a friend?"

I nodded, told her about Jessie, about the twenty-first birthday party, which was beginning now to seem so far away in time. Benjamin, smiling at me across the room. Jessie, in a buttercup jumpsuit, Drago's brilliant eyes staring into mine, her hoarse voice whispering about love, wealth, and the future. It made me feel good to think about it, to talk about it. As if it was a wonderful memory, long left behind.

Helen fidgeted. She brushed her wispy hair, then tousled it into fresh wisps. She said, "But you aren't really twenty-one yet, Gaby."

I smiled. "Almost. Just three weeks to go."

"And you fell in love with Benjamin," Helen said thoughtfully.

"Just like that." I looked down at the solitaire on my finger. "He was across the room. I was so aware of him. I kept watching him, wanting to meet him. I kept hoping. . . ."

"And then?"

"We met. Benjamin realized who I was almost at once."

"From the name, of course," Helen said. "It must have been that. He'd hardly recognize you in any other way."

I nodded. "Yes, of course."

"And you? Did you know him?"

I shook my head, brushed the curls off my forehead. "I didn't. I thought, for just a minute, that he looked familiar to me. But then I couldn't remember why, or from where, and I guess I forgot it. When we started to talk, and he explained, then I realized that I must have known him when I was a child."

"When you were ten," Helen said. "And he was eighteen."

"It was a long time ago."

"I'm sure it seems that way to you." Helen sighed again, shifted in the rockingchair. "And you fell in love so quickly, Gaby? Was that it? Or did you just decide you wanted to come to where you belong, come back to Cornell House?"

"I fell in love," I told her. "Otherwise . . . why, otherwise, I'd never have come here. I had no reason to. I hardly remembered my life here, you know. I never thought of it, or that I belonged here."

"You don't," Helen said softly. "You oughtn't to have come. You oughtn't to have promised to marry Benjamin Haley."

Her soft voice was clear, cool, full of unspoken menace. I couldn't understand it. Helen had always loved me. I knew that. I remembered it.

I swallowed hard, asked, "But why not?"

She gave the empty room a quick glance. When she spoke her voice was even softer. "Love, can't you see how this place has changed. Don't you understand what it means?"

"No, no, there are differences of course, but. . . ."

"We are none of us the people we used to be," Helen whispered. "I spoke out of turn earlier, talking against the marriage to Benjamin. I'm speaking out of turn now. But, love, it's not right." Her voice suddenly firmed. She sat very still. It was as if she had just had a satisfying thought. She said, "You're cousin to Benjamin, don't you see. Some kind of third cousin, I think it is. Yes, yes, that's it. I don't believe cousins should marry. It's against the Bible and against nature. And it's not healthy besides. Cousins oughtn't to marry. Your mother would say the same thing."

I considered briefly, then grinned, "Helen, dear, you know just as well as I do that we're not close enough for that to matter."

"You're too close," she said firmly. She began to rock hard. Then she asked, "Do you remember William?"

I shook my head.

"That's right. You wouldn't. Well, no matter. He's just arrived. Very unusual, too. I don't think he cares for this place much, nor for the changes that have taken place in it. But he's just arrived, picked this time to come for a visit. He's another some sort of third cousin of yours. But he's a Tysson, at least." She got to her feet, made a great rush for the door. She turned, whispered, "Gaby, love, if you were wise, you'd do what your mother did. It was hard for poor Rosalie, but she did it. You would steal away in the night and go as far as you can as fast as you can."

I asked quietly, "But why, Helen? Why did she do that?"

She eased the door open, gave the corridor a quick look, then she turned back, said, "Didn't she ever tell you?"

"She said only that she didn't want to live here after my father died."

Helen took a deep, shaky breath. At last she answered, "Then that's the reason. And it's a good enough reason for you, too."

"But Benjamin. . . ."

"Benjamin can take care of himself, Gaby. He always has and he always will. He's a true Haley, and don't you ever forget it."

You will find love, Drago whispered hoarsely. Oh, yes. Love, and great fortune, and happiness. There will be a tall, dark man, and a long life. You have had losses, and sorrow, and loneliness, but they are all behind you now. Now there will only be love. Her black eyes glowed and her red lips twisted over the sweet words as if they tasted bitter. Love, fortune, happiness and hope. And. . . . Her voice became even more hoarse, almost a raven's croak,

And you will lose them all, Gaby Tysson. You will know them and lose them and sink sadly and weeping into death. Just like your mother did.

"Oh, no," I screamed. "Oh, no, no. Jessie, stop her. Jessie don't let her say those terrible things. Jessie. . . ."

I struggled out of the bedclothes, fought myself free of their restraints.

I stared around the dark, unfamiliar room. It was a prison now. I was confined here against my will to suffer agonies I couldn't imagine. I thought I heard the fading echo of my cry in the silence. I tried to cling to the fading memory of the dream, but it slipped away beneath the scrutiny of consciousness. I knew only that Drago, the gypsy, had been about to warn me. The bright promise of the future had been tarnished by terror.

I climbed from bed, shivering. I tiptoed across the room, the carpet luxurious under my feet. It seemed to me a familiar sensation. Had I, as a child, been awakened from a bad dream? Had I tiptoed thus across the room to the window?

The terraces were silvered by moonlight. The pines were still sentinels against the sky. A yellow glow framed a window in Cornell Cottage.

I wondered if Benjamin were wakeful, too, and thinking of me. I wished that I dared slip into a robe, go down to him. But I couldn't imagine myself moving through the dark, still house, following the path down to the cottage, possibly to face the hard, cold, surprised stares of Johanna and Terrell. They, or one of them, might open the door to my knock. I might have to ask for Benjamin. What could I say?

I sighed, turned back to my bed.

It had begun so happily. Benjamin had come into

my life on the most joyful night I could remember, and he had brought love with him, and even more joy. But now, like a tiny worm in an apple, uneasiness gnawed at my hopes.

Drago had promised me love, happiness, I must cling to that. But the memory of the dream returned. Drago had promised me sorrow and death—but in the dream, only in the dream. I told myself that I mustn't allow a foolish dream to trouble me. Benjamin and I loved each other. We would marry and live happily ever after.

But I wondered if the dream had been the product of some awakened intuition.

Drago's prophecy had been hers.

The dream was mine.

It was a long time before I fell asleep again.

"So you're Gabriella Tysson."

The voice was deep and slow, and peculiarly underlined with amusement. I recognized it instantly. I had heard it for a few moments only the night before, but I knew it would be familiar for the rest of my life.

I looked up from the coffee Helen had served me just a little while earlier. I wished I had company. I didn't want to confront this man alone, although I didn't know why. He seemed presentable enough. He was heavy shouldered, as I'd seen in my glimpse of him the night before, tall. His hair was thick and sandy in color, but cut very short. His direct gaze was strange. I thought it must be because his eyes were so pale a gray that they seemed silver. He wore a blue, open necked shirt, with the sleeves rolled to his elbows, revealing muscled arms. His trousers were faded denim that had plainly seen years of wear.

"They call you Gaby, don't they?" he said, a faint color touching his tanned cheeks under my too-prolonged stare.

"Yes," I told him. "That's what everyone calls me." I smiled faintly. "I know that you're William Tysson. I heard you arrive last night."

"May I join you?"

"Oh. Of course. I'm sorry. I just didn't think. . . ."

He grinned at me. "Never mind." He sat down across from me, leaned his elbows on the table. "You must have heard Fernetta. My one man welcoming committee."

I nodded.

"They said you were sleeping."

"Just resting."

"Reunions are so tiring, aren't they?"

There was a quizzical amusement in his voice that made me uncomfortable. I answered finally, "I don't really know. I haven't had all that many."

He began a reply, then stopped it. He turned his head as the door swung open, and Helen appeared there.

He had a straight, hard profile, a sharp, high bridged nose, a square chin. His head was well-shaped and strong looking. I jerked my gaze away from him, embarrassed to find myself studying him so intently.

Helen gave him a quick, warm good morning, and put a coffee mug before him. Then she said, "You've met, have you?"

I nodded.

"You must have a long talk," she said, giving him a meaningful look.

"We will," he assured her.

I pretended to ignore that exchange. I didn't know what we would ever find to talk about. We were strangers, and had always been strangers, I was sure. I was just as sure that I preferred to leave it that way.

But Helen said earnestly, "You must listen to William, Gaby. He's the wise one in the family. He's been out in the world for years. He. . . ."

William cut in, laughing, "You're overselling me, Helen."

She gave him a warning glance. "I'll leave you to it. Remember the others will start trailing in fairly soon."

I couldn't finish my coffee. I found myself bracing for what was to come.

He said, "You really don't remember me, do you?"

I shook my head. "I'm sure I've never seen you before."

"Are you?" Amusement glinted in his silver eyes. "What if I told you that you had seen me, though."

"I'd believe you mistaken."

"And if I proved it?"

"I'd be very surprised."

"Don't be, Gaby. I'm thirty years old now. The last time you saw me I was twenty. You yourself were ten. It was at your father's funeral. A bad day that, and the weather made it even worse, if that was possible. The way the heavens opened up and the rain poured."

I stared into his silver eyes. I drew a deep breath. I wondered what he was trying to do to me, who he was, what he wanted. I gathered my courage and said firmly, "It didn't rain. I don't believe you were there."

"It didn't rain?" He studied me over the rim of his coffee mug. "You're sure, are you?"

"The sun was terribly bright. I couldn't bear it. It was as if my father's death were unimportant. I thought the heavens should fall down at least."

He sighed, said, "Perhaps you're right. That it wasn't raining, I mean. But there was a huge crowd afterwards. Here at the house. The whole family gathered to pay its respects."

I gave him a quick, hard look. My throat felt tight. As I said coldly, "I don't remember anybody. Just my mother and me. Uncle Bernard and Aunt Sally. I guess the Haleys must have been there, but I'm not sure."

They had gathered in the study. Those I mentioned, and yes, someone else—Joshua Horn, my father's elderly friend. They had been there, and several other men. I hadn't known what their preoccupation was about. But they had all been grim.

"What is it?" William was asking.

"I just remembered someone I want to see."

"Oh?"

"Joshua Horn. Do you know him?"

"I know him." William's narrowed eyes glinted. "Benjamin's clever," he said softly.

I stared at William.

He went on, "He cued you well, didn't he?"

6

"CUED ME WELL?" I echoed. "What are you talking about?"

His silver eyes swept me. I was suddenly conscious of my plain white shirt, blue jeans. I wished I had put on a dress. I wished I had been able to subdue my curls, and had put on more makeup. I felt that I needed such support for my dignity, and for my safety as well.

"You really don't know?" he asked.

I shook my head.

"Perhaps you'd better ask Benjamin." William set down his mug. "Tell me, would you be able to prove your identity if I were to ask that you should?"

"But everybody knows me," I cried. "I think you're crazy to ask me such a thing."

"But could you?"

"Helen's known me all my life." I took a deep angry breath. "Just ask her. See what she says."

"Helen's a quite elderly lady. She loved Gabriella Tysson. She wants to believe in Gabriella's return."

"And Sally, Bernard. Surely they. . . ."

"Sally is . . . well, can one depend on her? And as for Bernard, well, the less said the better."

I sputtered angrily, "You have no right to come here, to accuse me. . . ." But I was thinking that I'd known all along that Sally and Bernard had seemed to think I was an imposter, and had only unwillingly accepted me. But who was William? How did he dare?

He ignored my protest. He sipped his coffee, then set it down. He launched into a cross examination that left me shaken and even more angry.

He began, "Where have you been these last ten years?"

"In the city," I said.

"Where did you live?"

"On Bayside Drive at first. Then we moved to Jessup Terrace."

"What schools did you go to?"

"Farley Elementary. Denton Junior High. Garveau High."

"And you always used your own name? Your father's name?"

"Of course I did. Why shouldn't I?" I demanded.

He didn't answer me. Instead he pressed on. "You never had any contact with the family, with any individual member of it?"

"Of course not. I hardly remembered the family, or anyone from here. Until I met Benjamin."

"Your mother told you nothing about it? About why she left?"

"Why are you asking me all these questions?" I demanded. "What are you driving at?"

Again he didn't answer me.

"Are you a lawyer?" I asked.

He smiled faintly. The sun wrinkles on his face changed expression. All the hard, suspicious sternness seemed to melt away. He looked friendly, and warm, and gentle. He said, "I've given you the right to do some asking on your own, I guess." Then, "I'm William Tysson. That much you know. I'm the grandson of your father's oldest uncle. There's no use in my giving names. You won't remember them and they'll only confuse you. That makes me some sort of a distant cousin, I suppose, of Fernetta's." He paused, then added slowly, "And of yours, of course."

"Everything you've asked me . . . the things you've said . . . they add up to. . . ." I watched him carefully. "You don't believe that I'm Gaby Tysson, do you?"

He waited for a long moment. Then he sighed, "But I *do* believe it," he said gently. "I didn't for a little while. It seemed too pat, too opportune. But I do believe it now."

"Pat? Opportune? Why should you say that? Why should I pretend to be someone I'm not?"

He shrugged.

"It has to do with Benjamin, doesn't it?"

"In a way. And that's enough of that. I've admitted that I was wrong. Gaby. I . . . I only wish now that I hadn't been."

"But why would Benjamin bring me home, pretending I was Gaby Tysson, if I weren't?"

"Ask him, Gaby."

I didn't answer, but I decided to myself that I would do just that.

William said, "In fact, I *was* at your father's funeral, and it was a beautiful day. As far as the weather was concerned."

I saw the truth then. He'd been testing me. Just as he'd tested me about what happened after the funeral.

"I don't remember you," I told him.

"You wouldn't have. You were very upset, and a child. I was a grown man, away at college then. In recent years I've been out of the country a lot. I'm a mining engineer and I go where the job takes me."

Benjamin came in at that moment. He came to me, pressed a kiss on my cheek. To William, he said, "I didn't expect to see you."

"It was an impulse. I thought I'd drop in for a few days."

"Good," Benjamin said, but he didn't sound truly pleased. There was tension between the two men.

Benjamin took a chair, asked me, "Have you told him our plans?"

"No, I. . . ."

"We've spoken of other things," William cut in.

"Such as?"

"The family. I was telling her how the two of us are related."

"You and Gaby?"

William answered, "We stand in blood just about as distant as you and she do. You're—well, let's see. How does it actually go? Johanna was a Tysson, the daughter of Denby's youngest uncle."

"I guess that's right," Benjamin said. "I've never bothered to think about it."

I had been pursuing my own thoughts meanwhile. What William had actually been doing was quizzing me, implying that Benjamin had brought a stand-in for Gabriella Tysson to Cornell House. I wanted to ask Benjamin what William had had in mind.

But that seemed the wrong moment. I decided to wait.

Benjamin said, "I never thought of you as part of the family, William. I suppose because you didn't grow up here, as I did." He smiled at me, "And as you did, darling."

"But I didn't," I protested.

"You should have. And if it hadn't been for your mother's hysteria, you would have."

"Her hysteria?" I demanded.

"That's what it must have been," Benjamin said insistently. "Why else would she have gone the way she did after Denby died? This was her home, after all. This her family. Yet she turned her back on it, on them."

"She might have had her reasons," William suggested quietly.

I found myself grateful to him, and agreeing with him. My mother hadn't been a hysterical kind of woman. She had run away, yes. She must have been frightened. She must have had cause to be frightened. But of what? Of whom?

I shivered remembering again the day Terrell and Bernard had carried my father's body in—her screams, his limp body and bloodstained head.

Benjamin was demanding, "What reasons could she have had?"

William got to his feet. "We'll never know now, will we?"

"Are you staying long?" Benjamin asked.

"I don't know. It depends." At the door, William paused to ask, "When are the nuptials to be?"

"We'll decide this morning," Benjamin answered. "Won't we, Gaby?"

"I guess so," I told him.

He laughed softly, brushed the smooth wave across his forehead. "I know so. There's no reason to wait."

"I can think of one," William dryly retorted, and disappeared down the hallway, leaving his words trailing behind him.

Benjamin grinned. "We've always been rivals, you know. He has to oppose me no matter what."

If there was ever to be time, this was it, I knew. Yet I couldn't seem to find the right words to ask why he would think that Benjamin might bring a pretender to Cornell House. At last I said, "He asked a lot of questions, Benjamin. He didn't think I'm me. I'm sure of that."

Benjamin's grin widened. "You convinced him, I trust."

"I suppose I did. If I didn't, then nothing would. But why would he think such a thing?"

"I told you, we've always been rivals. He expects me to be up to something, no matter what."

"I felt certain he had something specific in mind," I insisted.

"I'm sure he did. One look at you, and he probably decided, and probably rightly, too, that I certainly don't deserve you."

I wanted to press the question, but I didn't see how I could.

Benjamin said, "Let's go for a ride this morning."

"I thought I'd write to Jessie today, and. . . ."

"You can do that any time. It's a beautiful day. I want to get you off all to myself. Do you realize we've had hardly a minute alone together since we got here yesterday afternoon?"

"I do realize it," I smiled.

We were on the way out to the terrace when Sally stopped me.

She put a thin, claw-like hand on my arm. Her eyes were bloodshot, and encircled with dark smudges. Her gray hair was hardly combed. She had on a green wrapper that could have stood a cleaning. The sight of her, so unkempt and worn looking, shocked me. She said, "Are you quite comfortably settled, Gaby?"

"Yes, I am, Aunt Sally," I told her.

"There's nothing you want? Nothing you need?"

"I don't think so."

"If there is, or should be, you must ask Helen. She'll see to it for you. She sees to everything, you know."

I thanked her.

"Where are you going now?"

"Out for a ride," Benjamin said. "I want to acquaint Gaby with the horses we have now."

Her pale lips tightened. She looked from me to Benjamin, then back to me. "You must be careful, Gaby. You haven't ridden for a long time." Then she went on, "We are, I don't know if you realized it yesterday, delighted to have you home with us again. It means so much to all of us."

"Thank you," I said again. But I thought that the words would have had more meaning to me if they had been delivered with any warmth or conviction. Spoken thus, coldly, as if memorized and then reeled off, I could only believe that what was conveyed was the opposite of what was felt. Still, that didn't seem to matter. Only Benjamin did. And perhaps, after we were married, I would make him see that we mustn't live with the family, with my aunt and uncle, with his parents. We must go off, on our own, and build our lives together. I supposed that was actually what he was planning, though he had never mentioned that to me.

I would, when we were riding this morning, bring it up, tell him how I felt.

At the cottage, Benjamin said he had to make a phone call, and would be right out. I sat down on the steps to wait.

That was when Terrell joined me.

He wore black high boots and tan breeches, and a tan shirt. The sun seemed to spotlight the patches of gray at his temples. Except for those he could have been a heavier, more weathered Benjamin.

He sat on the steps beside me, and asked, with a faint, tilted smile, "Are they treating you all right at the house?"

"Oh, yes. Everything's fine."

"I hear William Tysson arrived last night."

I nodded.

"You've spoken to him?"

Once again I nodded.

Terrell's tilted smile grew. "He's a fine man, Gaby. But I'm afraid he's always resented us Haleys somewhat."

"But why should he?" I asked, thinking that here I might find the explanation for the peculiar interview I had just had with him.

Terrell shrugged his muscular shoulders. "I suppose it's because of my position here. It's Bernard's place and responsibility. But I help him run it. He needs that help, you know. He isn't a well man, hasn't been for years. I suppose you remember."

I shook my head. My uncle had always seemed perfectly healthy to me. Then I remembered I had seen him, so many years before, with his face bandaged, staggering beneath Terrell's guiding hand while Johanna stood by, watching. I remembered the red scar on his forehead. Perhaps at that time he had received an injury. . . .

Terrell went on, "And since Fernetta's terrible accident, you see, he just hasn't been the same."

"Yes," I agreed, because I didn't know what else to say.

He went on, "I hope you weren't put off by us yesterday, Gaby. We were just shocked. I'm sure you understand. That you should turn up, out of the blue, so to speak, and then Benjamin's. . . ."

I turned, looked at the door behind me, wondering what was keeping Benjamin.

"Lover's impatience," Terrell grinned. "He'll be out in a minute. I just want you to know that you belong here."

I didn't answer him. I was more and more sure that I must convince Benjamin otherwise. I didn't belong in Cornell House and never would. All I wanted was to marry Benjamin and go away with him.

Terrell went on, "I understand that you're going out riding."

"Yes," I agreed uneasily. The closer the time came, the less enthusiastic I felt, and I had begun with little enthusiasm at best.

"Do you know horses well?"

"I haven't been near one since I was ten years old." I paused, then confessed, "And I'm not even sure I want to try again. But Benjamin says I couldn't have forgotten how to ride. I hope he's right."

"He is. But I'll give you a steady old nag. You needn't worry."

As he got to his feet, Bernard came hurrying down

the path. His hair was tousled. His clothes were disheveled, as if he had hurriedly climbed into them. The scar glowed on his forehead.

"What are you doing?" he demanded.

Terrell stared at him coolly. "What's the matter, Bernard? Have you had a bad dream? You look only half awake and half in your senses."

Bernard sat heavily on the steps beside me. He put his plump hands on his knees. He said, "I'm going to drive to . . . well, down to the highway in a couple of minutes. Want to come?"

"She's going riding with Bernard," Terrell told him coolly.

"Riding?" Bernard peered at me. "You still ride?"

"I don't know. I'm going to try."

"Foolish to do it after so long. You never know . . . you never know. . . ."

Terrell said silkily, "Bernard, are you trying to make me feel guilty about Fernetta? You know exactly what happened. You know. . . ."

Bernard's face flamed. He got to his feet. "I didn't mean that, Terrell. I just thought. . . ."

"Of course you didn't," Terrell agreed silkily.

Bernard paced a few steps, then paced back. "Be careful, Gaby."

"I'm putting her on Nellie," Terrell laughed. "Not on Devil's Dancer. There's nothing to worry about."

Fernetta called from the terrace, then she and William came down together.

They greeted me, the others, then Fernetta asked, "Where's Benjamin?"

"He'll be right out," Terrell said.

There was something oddly reminiscent in that moment. I couldn't think what it was. Terrell disappeared into the stable, then came out leading a broadbacked horse.

"Come on," he told me. "Give old Nellie a pat, and we'll saddle her up for you."

I touched Nellie's nose timidly. She snapped her tail and I fell back.

Terrell laughed. "She won't bite. Let her know who's boss."

"I'm afraid she'll find out that she is," I said.

He went back into the stables, then returned with a heavy saddle.

He and Bernard set it on Nellie's back, and worked over it, fussing with straps and buckles. The horse moved restively while they cinched and shortened the stirrups.

Terrell said, "You're a little thing, Gaby. Hardly bigger than when you were a child the last time I saw you." He gave me another tilted smile that reminded me of Benjamin. "Doesn't all this seem familiar? Me getting the horse ready for you?"

I gave him a bewildered glance. "I don't know. Should it?"

"I did it often enough. For you. For you and your father, too, you know. Back then, in those years. . . ."

Bernard, the scar flaming, said thickly, "How would she know about that?"

Johanna came out of the cottage then. She smiled coolly at me, said, "Benjamin will be just a minute more. I had him get something from the attic for me when he finished his phone call and it took him longer to find than I thought, and longer than he wanted, too."

"I'm glad to have a minute to talk to Gaby before Benjamin rushes her off," Terrell replied.

"You're always glad to talk to a pretty girl."

"Particularly one that's soon to be my daughter-in-law," he retorted.

Fernetta had been so quiet, for so long, that I turned to look at her. She was huddled in the wheelchair, her hands white knuckled. Her face was pale, shrunken. Her wide open blue eyes were shadowed. I felt pity well up in me. I knew that she was wishing she could still be active, could climb into the saddle and ride away on Nellie. Ride away with Benjamin. But I didn't know what to say to her, nor how I could offer comfort.

William left her, walked slowly around Nellie, brows raised, silver eyes amused. "Where did you get this old bag of glue, Terrell?"

"She wasn't always that way. I've just kept her. Sentimental value, you know."

"I always wondered," William said, fingering the saddle, "just what happened to Satan's Son. He was such a fine animal. Did you sell him?"

There was a brief silence. Then Terrell answered shortly, "We destroyed him. After what happened. . . ." He glanced sideways at me, then looked away quickly, and I knew he was wondering if I recalled that Satan's Son was the horse that had thrown my father to his death. "After what happened," Terrell repeated, "we just didn't want him around."

"A pity," William said lightly. "He was a fine animal."

"You wouldn't have known. He went bad. He turned killer."

"I wouldn't have thought so," William answered.

At that moment Benjamin came out, breathless with apologies. "I'm sorry, Gaby."

"I explained," Johanna told him, and went into the cottage.

Fernetta's eyes were fixed anxiously on Benjamin's face.

I was glad that he noticed, glad that he said, "Good morning, Fernetta. You're down early, aren't you?"

"I couldn't sleep somehow."

"You don't look the worse for it, I must say."

Her pale face flushed. Her eyes brightened, but the anxious look remained. "You'll be careful, won't you? The both of you?"

Benjamin said gently, "Of course, Fernetta."

He turned to me. "Ready?"

I was as ready, I supposed, as I would ever be. I didn't tell him that. Instead, I nodded.

He helped me mount, put the reins in my hands. The touch of our fingers gave me a quick reassurance. I sat up straight and still, feeling Nellie quiver under me.

Terrell had brought out the huge black stallion that I knew must be Devil's Dancer.

Benjamin swung into the saddle, and the horse reared and kicked, but Benjamin soon brought him under control.

We moved off slowly together. I was conscious of the others watching us. Fernetta, tense and silent. William, thoughtful. Terrell, smiling faintly. Bernard, red faced and breathing hard.

I was relieved when we left them behind, more relieved that I could relax to Nellie's long, smooth, careful stride.

"It's going to be okay," I said happily.

"Of course. What did you think?"

We walked across the golden meadows. On the right, the jagged teeth of the cliffs rose against the sky. On the left, the fields sloped upward along the mountainsides. The tall dark pines relieved the monotony, casting long early shadows.

Benjamin smiled at me. "What do you think, Gaby? Shall we get married tomorrow? The day after?"

It was what I wanted, but now that he had put it into words I felt uneasy. I didn't like the sensation of being swept along on swift currents I had just discovered. I said, "We should first have some place to live, Benjamin."

"But we do. Right here."

"We should be on our own when we're married."

Devil's Dancer suddenly reared and sidestepped. Benjamin swore at him, jerked at the bit. "He wants a good run, that's what's eating at him." Then, "But this is your home, our home, Gaby."

"No, Benjamin. It isn't, and can't be."

"I'm sorry. They haven't made you feel welcome, I suppose. I oughtn't to have exposed you to their peculiarities. But it isn't you, you know. I've already explained. My folks are pretty possessive, and as for Sally and Bernard, well, you can see how they are about Fernetta."

I knew he was right. The Haleys and Tyssons both had their own separate reasons for resenting my return to Cornell House.

But I couldn't bear the thought of beginning my life with him among people who resented me. Perhaps if they knew me better, if they could grow to like me, then. . . .

I said, "Would you be terribly angry if I suggested that we wait?"

Devil's Dancer reared again, and he swore.

I added quickly, raising my voice so he could hear me, "Just for a week or so?"

He pulled the horse to a stop.

Nellie moved on slowly. I had forgotten to signal her.

Benjamin caught up with me. He grinned. "Okay, Gaby. Next week it is."

There were drumming hooves, a hail, from the edge of the meadow. We both turned.

Terrell yelled, "Long distance call, Benjamin. It may be important."

Benjamin groaned, shouted to his father, "I'm coming. Tell them to hold on." Then, to me, "You go on. Give Nellie her head. She'll know the way, and I'll catch up in a minute."

I tried to protest, but he slapped Nellie's rump with his hand. She moved off slowly. He turned, galloped back toward the cottage.

Nellie went on. It was pleasant. The rhythm of the gait was smooth and slow. The saddle felt comfortable beneath me. I was remembering long rides with my father. He had always stuck close to me. There had been dogs trotting along beside us.

Then, suddenly, I found that I had to clench my legs tighter and tighter around Nellie's broad back. I had to thrust harder and harder to keep my toes in the stirrups.

Nellie stopped for no reason I knew. She flicked her tail, and shook herself hard, and then took off at a fast gallop.

The reins pulled from my cold fingers. I fell forward over the saddle, and felt it sliding from under me as my feet lost the stirrups. I flung my arms around Nellie's neck, fingers clenching her mane, and held on for dear life.

But I couldn't hold on for long.

7

THE SKY SEEMED to spin around me. I felt myself fly in the air for a long time. I seemed to hang there, suspended between life and death, and I heard my father's voice, remembered from long before, telling me to relax and let go, telling me to roll.

His voice was still in my ears when I hit the ground. The shock jolted the breath from my lungs, jolted every bone in my body. I rolled and kept rolling, and at last I sprawled limp and still, with the earth quivering under me.

In that instant I immediately relived the terrible ride, the saddle slipping from beneath me, the stirrups gone, the wild thud of Nellie's hooves. I relived it, and felt the mists of death swirl around me.

That was when I realized that I had lived all my life before in a protracted dream. I had assumed always that there lay ahead of me safety and happiness. When I heard Drago's hoarse words I had believed them because I had expected them to be true. Now I knew of the imminence of death. Now I knew terror.

That recognition took only an instant, yet it seemed to go on for eons. It became a part of me as I dragged myself to a sitting position, fighting away the mists of panic.

I cringed at the sound of thudding hooves, thinking Nellie had come back to trample me.

But William burst from the shadows. He threw himself off a strawberry roan, knelt beside me. "Gaby, what happened?"

"I don't know," I said bleakly. "Nellie bolted and threw me."

He bent closer. His strong square hands brushed my arms, legs, felt my shoulders, my neck. His touch was strangely comforting, and that embarrassed me. I drew away.

He seemed to understand. He said quickly, "I was checking for broken bones. I think you're all right." He grinned faintly then, and I realized, when I saw color return to it, that his face had been pale. "Except for some bruises, I mean. And it looks as if you've ripped your knees."

With him helping me, I got to my feet gingerly. I found that I could stand. When I had caught my breath, I found that I could walk.

I said, "It was crazy, the way it happened."

"You haven't ridden for so long. Your balance, maybe...."

But it had been more than that, I was sure. Nellie had danced wildly, then taken off. The saddle had slipped from under me.

William was staring at me. "Gaby, what do you think happened? The way you look, sound...."

But I had no reason to trust him, no reason to tell him what I suspected.

I was determined to find Nellie, to examine her, her saddle.

But William insisted on taking me back to the house, promising that then he would find Nellie and return her to the stable.

As we went slowly across the meadow, I wondered if he had any special reason to keep me from finding Nellie.

But when we reached the corral, she was waiting, patiently nuzzling the gate.

"At least she knows her way home," William said. She ignored me. I caught up her reins, and she flicked her tail. I smoothed the rumpled blanket on her back, and felt something sharp gouge my finger. I winced, and Nellie moved, but I managed to palm the small sharp object. William was examining the saddle, head bent, eyes narrow. I took a quick look at my palm. It held a long, thin, rusty nail. I slipped it into my pocket.

Now the terror that I had learned tumbling through empty air had become real.

Someone had put the nail under the blanket, knowing that Nellie would eventually feel it digging into her hide, knowing that she would dance and run, and that I, inexperienced as I was, would surely fall.

But who could have done it?

They had all been at the corral with me. Terrell had saddled Nellie with Bernard's help. William had walked around her, stood beside her. And Benjamin. . . .

Now he came running from the cottage. "Gaby! What's the matter?"

I swallowed, my throat dry, my lips parched.

"She had a fall," William said.

"Oh, darling." Benjamin came to me quickly, his dark brows drawn with concern. "It's my fault. I oughtn't to have come back to take the phone call and let you go off alone. But I was sure you'd be all right. Nellie's a pet. She couldn't possibly have done anything to unseat you."

"But she did," William answered. "She spooked and ran away."

"Why didn't you hang on?" Benjamin asked. "Surely you remembered that much."

"I couldn't," I told him briefly.

Benjamin's arms closed around me. I felt as if I couldn't move, breathe. He said, "Come on, darling, let's get you cleaned up. I'll give you a chance to get your land legs and we'll try again tomorrow."

I didn't tell him then that I'd never ride again. I allowed him to lead me up the path toward the house.

Every step of the way I was conscious of William's silver gaze, following after us.

Fernetta, crouched in her wheelchair, was on the upper terrace, sitting in the shadow of an umbrella. Her face was white and still as she watched my approach.

I wondered what she was thinking.

Benjamin said lightly, "Gabys had a small fall, but she's okay."

Fernetta whispered, "A fall? From Nellie?" Her hands squeezed the arms of the wheelchair. She turned beseeching blue eyes on me. "Gaby, what happened?"

"It was nothing," I told her.

"Nothing this time maybe." Her voice was hoarse, bitter. "What about next time?"

Benjamin said gently, "That's enough, Fernetta. We don't need your play acting and self-drama now."

"Play acting?" Fernetta cried. "Am I play acting in this chair? Have I been play acting for the past two years?"

I intervened quickly, "Fernetta, Benjamin didn't mean that. He's just so worried about me that he doesn't know what he's saying."

"But I do," Benjamin contradicted me. "I don't think this is the time for Fernetta to begin her tale of woe. Her troubles are in the past. Yours are right now. You need some ice on your knees, and tapes, and a chance to catch your breath. And I mean to see that you get them without delay."

He brushed past Fernetta, drawing me with him.

I looked back at her. She was watching us. Her blue eyes glistened. Tears shone on her cheeks. My heart ached for her.

She said through quivering lips, "Gaby, just remember one thing. Your father died when he fell from Satan's Son. I injured my spine when I fell from Quick Canter. You've had your fall. Don't take your life in your hands again."

Benjamin made an impatient sound, hurrying me along the hallway. I wished I had been able to reassure her. But there was no time, and it wasn't the right time anyway. I looked sideways at Benjamin. There was a cold hard set to his mouth. His dark eyes were narrowed. His jaw was tightly clenched, forcing a play of small muscles.

I pulled at his arm. "I'm stiff and bruised, Benjamin. I can't hurry so."

"I want to get you away from Fernetta's hysterical

talk. I don't want you upset by her. The girl is frantic with her disability. Half the time she doesn't know what she's talking about. The other half she's so jealous of you she'd do anything to drive you away."

Jealous, perhaps. I knew that she loved Benjamin. I had seen how anxiously her eyes followed him, how she responded to the small atentions he paid her. But what she had said had been a warning to me. A reminder of the past. A prophecy of the future. And she didn't know about the nail under the horse blanket. She didn't know how the saddle had slipped away from under me. I reminded myself that her festering resentment against Terrell, her blaming him for her accident, might be a product of her crippling. It might be that she had to blame someone, anyone. It might be that her warning was a result of the disorder of her mind.

The nail in my pocket was real. I touched it, and it was still there.

Benjamin led me into my room, pressed me into a chair.

"I'm all right," I told him. "Don't fuss so."

"You're more hardy than you look," he grinned, pleased with me.

I was more hardy than I had thought, too. I had found a strength and determination I hadn't known existed in me since my fall from Nellie. I touched the nail in my pocket again. It was proof. It told me what I might never have known, never been sure of. The strange coldness of my welcome to Cornell House had been no mere matter of possessiveness or jealousy, of childish emotions I could dissipate by making myself loved. I had an enemy here. An enemy prepared to kill.

My father had died. . . .

My mother had run away, hidden. . . .

Fernetta had been injured. . . .

Now there had been an attempt on me. I could not now see a pattern, link these things together. But I vowed to myself that I would. For my love for Benjamin, I would.

I said only, "Benjamin, please do go away. I want to wash the dust off, and change my clothes."

"I'll send Helen to help you."

"I don't need any help."

"Just to please me? So I'll feel better?"

"For you then," I said smiling. "If it *will* make you feel better."

"It will. But only a little. Do you realize how it is when I think that I took for granted that you could ride alone? That I let you go off, just to take a silly phone call? When I should have been with you?"

"But it doesn't matter, Benjamin. Nothing happened."

When he had left me though, I thought of Fernetta's words again. Of the three accidents that perhaps were not accidents. I looked at the nail. I couldn't see how it could have gotten under Nellie's blanket unless someone had put it there. Then what happened to me was no accident.

What of the two others?

Had my mother had her own unspoken suspicions? Her weeping words, "It couldn't have happened. Not to Denby! It couldn't have!" had been an accusation that I still remembered. Was that why she had taken me and slipped away immediately after my father was buried? Was that why she had never returned to Cornell House, nor even spoken of it?

Helen came scurrying in, her gray-white hair

wispy as ever, her blue eyes shadowed with worry. But she managed to make her voice casual, saying, "Benjamin told me about it. What an odd thing. I hope you're really all right, love."

I slipped the nail into a dresser drawer, assured her that all I needed was a hot soak in the tub.

"He says you're not nearly as frail as I think. But that's what he wants to believe," Helen told me.

She surveyed my scratched knees, clicked her tongue, and went off to get cloths. Returning quickly, she hustled me out of my jeans, and worked over the cuts. Then she drew a bath for me and left me to it. I wasn't accustomed to that much pampering, and told her so.

Her blue eyes looked even more shadowed. "But you should be, love." Before I could answer, she said, "You soak, and I'll bring you a tea tray. There's nothing like a good hot cup of tea to steady the nerves."

I knew I mustn't argue with her. She wanted to do something. So I agreed that I would enjoy some tea, and settled into my bath.

I let myself sink into the hot, scented water, trying to relax my tense muscles. I lay back, refusing to think, but the small worm of unease that had marred my coming here with Benjamin had turned into the coiling snake of fear. I felt it crowd in on me. I stepped from the tub, dried myself, powdered, and pulled on a robe.

Helen was setting a tea tray on the table. She poured from a fine blue China pot into a fine blue China cup. She eased thinly sliced buttered bread towards me.

I thanked her, sipped at the tea.

She said, "I forgot, in all the excitement. But Joshua Horn was here."

For a moment, I didn't recognize the name. But then I remembered. I had thought of him before. My father's old friend. He had been there, after the funeral, with a couple of other men.

"I wish I hadn't missed him," I said. "I'd like to see him."

"Then you do remember him, Gaby?"

I nodded.

"He asks that you return his call. I do think you should do that."

There was a tense undertone in her voice. It made me wonder.

I asked, "For some special reason?"

She didn't answer immediately. She fidgeted with her hair, her glasses. She twitched her skirt. At last she said, "It would be the polite thing to do. He was such a good friend in the old days. And he's wise. And ... well, it would please him."

"Didn't he say he'd stop back?"

"No. And I shouldn't wait, if I were you. If I were you I would go today."

"Perhaps I will."

"Do it," Helen urged, looking at me sideways through her glasses.

"But why is it so important?"

Helen shrugged. "Good manners are important, love. Now aren't they? Aren't they?"

I was about to agree with her, with reservations, when the door burst open.

I quickly tugged the robe tighter around me.

Bernard paused on the threshold, then trotted across the room to me. His face was red, the scar glowing on his forehead. His breath rattled in his throat.

"What's this? What's this?" he demanded. "Fernetta's been saying that you had an accident, Gaby."

Sally came after him. She wore a pair of trousers that hung on her flat body, a shirt that seemed three sizes too big at the shoulders. She said softly, "Now, Bernard, just wait a minute. Just don't get excited, Bernard. Just wait and see. . . ."

"Look at me," I said quickly. "I'm fine. Can't you see? I'm just fine."

Bernard's thick body crumpled into a chair as if his legs would no longer hold him. He let his head fall back against the cushions. "Fernetta! The way she talked. . . ."

Was his relief feigned, I wondered.

He had been in the stables with Terrell. He had walked around Nellie, been close to her, just as William had been. Which of the three men could have slipped the nail under the saddle blanket?

Sally said, "You see? It was nothing. I told you. . . ."

Bernard cut her off with a quick, sour look. "Do be still," he ordered, when her voice continued and he saw the look wouldn't suffice.

She subsided, twisting thin and shaking hands nervously.

Bernard peered at me. "Now then, I want you to tell me all about it."

"But there's nothing to tell," I protested. "I just fell. Nellie ran away with me. I should have held on tighter. . . ."

"You're my brother's only child," he said heavily. "You're all that's left of him. I have the right to know. You must tell me the truth."

"I have," I said.

And he accepted the lie. A deep sigh rasped in his throat. "So that's all it was?"

"Of course. It could have happened to anyone. Especially a novice like me."

Bernard and Sally exchanged glances.

Finally Bernard said, "You used to ride like the wind. You learned about the time that you could walk. Could you have forgotten. . . ."

I knew that once again they were thinking that I might not be Gabriella Tysson. They were hoping that I might not be. I didn't care. I refused to argue with them. I said only, "That was years ago. I've forgotten all I ever knew, obviously."

"Then you mustn't ride any more," Bernard said. "I'll speak to Terrell and Benjamin about it. We don't want anything to happen to you, you know."

"Bernard!" Sally wailed.

His color faded. The scar stood out.

And I suddenly remembered the first time I'd seen it. I saw him, bandaged, shaky on his feet, with Johanna on one side of him, and Terrell on the other. I heard Sally wail, "Bernard!" My father was there, too. His blond head shone in the sunlight, but his face was grim. "That's the last time you go to Las Vegas, Bernard," he said quietly. I remembered being sent away, and the grownups huddled in whispered talk.

Now Bernard got to his feet, went to the door. His color had returned to normal. He said quietly, "I feel that you're my responsibility, Gaby. As long as you're in Cornell House. So I worry about you."

Sally, like a tiny tug trying to move a huge barge, nudged him into the hallway. "Never mind, Bernard. The girl's not really listening to you. Don't you see? Don't you understand? There's nothing you can do."

"I can," he said tiredly. "I will."

"Oh, why did you come?" Sally cried to me. "Why did you have to come back?"

I was dressing when Fernetta rolled herself into my room.

She looked me up and down carefully. Then she said, using her mother's words, "Why did you come back, Gaby? Why do you stay?"

I finished buttoning my pale green blouse, then tucked it into the full skirt I had put on earlier. I sat on the edge of the bed. "Fernetta, you know why. Benjamin and I are to be married. He lives here. He wants. . . ."

She shook back her long, dark hair. Her face looked pinched and tired. "But you see how it's changed."

I didn't answer her. I waited.

"I don't mean Johanna's pool. I don't mean that Terrell got rid of all the dogs."

I continued to wait.

"Gaby, don't you realize what's happened? My mother's become nothing more than a shivering drunk. And my father's a great hulk of nothing. Nobody's happy here any more. They're all afraid. They're afraid, Gaby, I tell you. And it's terrible to be afraid."

I didn't say so aloud, but I thought, Yes, yes, it's a terrible thing to be afraid.

8

WHAT HAD BENJAMIN brought me to? I asked myself as I went downstairs.

Who was my enemy?

Terrell? Bernard? William? Or was it Benjamin himself?

The suspicion shook me, filled me with pain.

No, no. It couldn't be Benjamin. We had fallen in love at first sight, and were in love now, soon, my fears behind me, we would be married.

The others were already at the dining room table. They greeted me with concern that I had not rested longer. I searched each face for a sign of guilt, a sign of disappointment. I saw nothing.

Benjamin drew a chair out for me, seated himself beside me.

There was a brief silence. I broke it, saying, "Helen told me that my father's old friend, Joshua Horn, was here to see me."

Terrell raised dark brows. "When you were out on your adventurous ride."

"I wish I'd known. I'd like to have seen him."

"You'd only just gone out," Terrell said. "And I didn't have a horse saddled. Benjamin suggested to me that I ought to let you go on, so Mr. Horn had a cup of tea with me, and then went home."

"He asked that I return the visit. I think I'd like to."

"Whatever for?" Johanna asked coolly. "You're already surrounded by middleaged and elderly. And Mr. Horn is really quite doddering by now."

"Besides," Bernard put in. "He'll be back."

"I doubt that," Terrell said. "We've seen him rarely these last ten years."

"He'll be back," Bernard repeated. "To see Denby's daughter."

Terrell chuckled. "Would you like to bet fifty dollars on that?"

There was a peculiar silence. Then Bernard answered, "You know that I am not a gambling man," and the scar stood out on his forehead.

Terrell chuckled again.

Sally said something. Johanna answered.

But I no longer listened. Gambling. The word had struck a chord.

Bernard had come back from one of his many trips to Las Vegas, his face bandaged, with Johanna and Terrell with him. But this time there had been some trouble. My father had been angry. Angry at Bernard, but angry at Terrell, too.

"Gaby?" Benjamin was asking.

I glanced at him.

He touched my hand. "Darling, you seem a thousand miles away."

"I was thinking about Mr. Horn."

"You needn't go today, you know."

"But I'd like to."

"Then I'll take you," William offered, his first words since I sat down.

Benjamin frowned. "I had other plans."

"We've plenty of time," I said, smiling.

"Do you remember Joshua Horn?" Sally asked, her thin, un-madeup face looking sickly in the bright, sun filled room.

"Just a little. He played chess with my father."

"It hardly seems a recommendation for a visit on a nice afternoon," Benjamin grinned. "I don't see you playing chess with a seventy-five-year-old man."

"I suppose Rosalie—your mother, I mean—spoke of him often."

I stared at her. "Never."

"Oh, really?"

I didn't answer that. I was aware of strange crosscurrents. They made me more than ever determined to see Joshua Horn. Perhaps he could explain them, explain Helen's insistence, too.

That, it turned out, was more easily decided than accomplished.

When lunch was finished, William repeated his offer to take me to Mr. Horn's, but Benjamin insisted that I must have a rest, and that then, he, Benjamin would escort me.

I spent half an hour looking at my wristwatch in my room and went downstairs. Then Benjamin said, "I can't see why you're so anxious to visit that dull old man."

"He might not be dull."

"I know him," Benjamin retorted. "He is."

I went in search of William, and found him at the

corral, thoughtfully staring at Nellie. He agreed to take me, but when we got into his car, and he turned the ignition, it wouldn't start.

He swore briefly and got out. He spent a little while fishing under the hood. Then he came and told me it would take him a little while to do a small repair job.

I sat inside, waiting for him.

It occurred to me, as I watched him work over the motor, the sun making his sandy hair bright, that he was the one person at Cornell House who didn't make me feel like a prisoner. Everyone else's smiling resistance to my wish to do as I pleased made me realize that though I had come as a guest, as a relative, I had become something other than that in the single day since my arrival.

I was totally dependent on Benjamin. I could not walk away from Cornell House. I didn't know how to drive. I wouldn't dare mount a horse again. I was at the mercy of every relative who lived there—at the mercy of William, too, in a sense.

It was a frightening thought.

I was determined not to allow it to continue. Somehow I would regain my freedom, be beholden to no one.

At last William appeared at the car window, wiping his hands.

"What was it?" I asked.

"Gas pump was disconnected." He put the rag away, closed the hood, then got in beside me. "You haven't changed your mind?"

"No. Why should I?"

"You must be determined, to wait so patiently for so long."

There was something in his voice that made me

ask, "Did someone tamper with the car, William? Or is it one of those things that happen."

"I don't know," he said, sliding a bright silver look at me. "But I'm a man who takes pretty good care of my car."

We drove the curving dirt road up to the crest, and then down the mountain to the highway. We rode only a short distance before we turned off on a dirt road and began to climb again.

Joshua Horn's house was just on the other side of the mountain from Cornell House, but it could be reached only through this circuitous route.

When we arrived, I was glad that William had brought me, that he had gone to the trouble of fixing the car.

The house was small, more window than white wood, topped with a red tiled roof. As we drove in and parked, an elderly man rose from a chaise on a wide porch.

He came down to meet us, and I knew him instantly.

He was small, withered, but lithe. He had a circlet of white hair on a mostly bald head. He had a quick, straight stride.

He stood, hands out, head cocked to one side, and surveyed me through velvety black eyes. "Gabriella," he said finally. "Of course. You *are* Gabriella. You could be no one else."

I heard the faint stress. It reminded me of my meeting with Sally and Bernard, with Johanna and Terrell. It reminded me of the session I'd had with William. They all of them had thought I might be an impostor. I once more wondered why.

"Yes," I said aloud. "I'm Gabriella, Mr. Horn."

He took my hand, his wrinkled fingers warm on my flesh. He drew me with him to the porch.

William followed, ungreeted and unremarked on. He might have been invisible.

Mr. Horn asked, "Do you remember me at all? Is that possible after this amount of time?"

"I thought you used to play chess with my father."

"I did. I did." He gave me a wide, delighted grin. "Then you do remember."

"Not very much though. Just that you had been to the house. And that last day. When my father was buried . . . afterwards, you, the family, some other men. . . ."

"The lawyers." He looked at William then.

William shook his head, said nothing.

Mr. Horn went on, "I never thought I'd see you again, Gabriella. Not at Cornell House. When Helen called and told me you had returned. . . ." He nodded his almost bald head. "I was surprised. More, I was. . . ."

"But why?" I asked.

"Why?"

I waited.

"More to the point, Gabriella, is why you have returned," he said softly.

"It was Benjamin," I explained.

"Benjamin Haley?"

William spoke for the first time. His voice was hard, impatient. He said. "He found her in the city."

Mr. Horn stared at William. "Benjamin found her? After all this time?"

"That's what she says," William answered.

"That's what's true," I said hotly.

William's jaw squared.

But Mr. Horn turned velvety eyes on me. "Would you like to tell me about it, Gabriella?"

"Why not? I have no reason to refuse to."

Mr. Horn smiled faintly. Then, "William, would you go inside? Could you make a pot of coffee? You'll find your way, I'm sure."

William gave Mr. Horn a quick hard look, but did as he was told. He rose, disappeared into the house.

I heard his firm stride fade away.

"Now then," said Mr. Horn, "Perhaps, this way, in private, you can speak more freely. But we won't have much time, will we?"

"I have nothing to hide from William Tysson, or from anyone else," I answered.

Mr. Horn sighed. "You met Benjamin how?"

I explained about my job and Jessie. I explained about the premature birthday party and my meeting with Benjamin.

"Your twenty-first birthday," he said. "Then that's why you came back."

"No. That's not why. It was because of Benjamin." I thrust my hand out, showed him the solitaire Benjamin had given me. "We're engaged to be married."

"And your birthday?"

"It's not until three weeks."

"And before then. . . ."

I had told Benjamin that we would be married within the week. Now I was no longer sure. I said, "Mr. Horn, we haven't quite decided. It won't be long though."

"And so you've known Benjamin Haley for what is it? Three days? Five?"

"Why, when I was a child, at Cornell House. . . ."

He stopped me by lifting a withered hand. "Gabriella, do you really remember him from that time?

Are you saying that you loved him when you were ten years old?"

I hesitated, then grinned. "No, no, of course not." I paused, then continued thoughtfully, "The truth is I hardly remember him, or any of the Haleys, from that time."

"For good reason, I can tell you. Gabriella, do you realize that the Haleys, with Benjamin, came to Cornell House just two weeks to the day before your father died?"

"Two weeks?" I murmured. "But I thought . . . somehow I imagined. . . ."

"That they'd always been there? Oh, no. Certainly not. Did he, they, allow you to think that?"

I didn't answer him. I wasn't sure. I felt somehow as if I were betraying Benjamin even by wondering. I said only, "Then that's why I hardly remember them, of course."

"It must be."

I wasn't sure, I couldn't remember now, just what Benjamin had told me. How it was that I had imagined that we had lived together when I was a child. But it didn't matter. I saw no way, then, in which it could matter. I had fallen in love with him, not because I had once known him, but because I knew him now.

Mr. Horn's velvety eyes were focused on something beyond my shoulder. I turned to look, and realized that he was staring at the mountain that separated us now from Cornell House.

He said, "They came, the Haleys, with your Uncle Bernard."

I leaned forward. "Mr. Horn, was that the time he was hurt?"

"Yes. He was in serious straits. An unpaid gambling debt. If Johanna and Terrell hadn't found him, taken care of him, brought him home. . . ."

"Gambling," I repeated, remembering Terrell's words at lunch that day, the offer to bet fifty dollars on Mr. Horn's return, and Bernard's angry refusal, his insistence that he didn't gamble. Terrell had been teasing Bernard, of course.

Now Mr. Horn said, "Why must you make a decision so soon that might affect your whole life, Gabriella?"

"I'm in love," I answered.

He replied with a seeming irrelevance. "Yes, they came back from Las Vegas together. Your father was very angry. Two weeks later he died. The Haleys stayed on. I began to feel myself unwelcome, though I persisted in visits for some years. Then I saw Bernard changing. I saw what happened to Sally. I'm an old man. I didn't know where your mother and you had gone. It seemed. . . ."

He stopped, and though I murmured to encourage him to continue, he remained silent.

"It has nothing to do with me," I said at last.

"Nothing," Mr. Horn murmured. "But you remain so young."

I tensed, leaned forward. "I know how I feel. And twenty-one isn't too young for marriage, is it?"

"Isn't it?" The voice was curt. It seemed to slap at me. William stood in the doorway, balancing a tray in his big hands. "I doubt that it's an age when a person knows everything there is to know."

"I know who I love," I said defensively.

He shrugged. He leaned over me, offering a cup of coffee. When I had taken it, thanked him stiffly, he served Mr. Horn. "Talk some sense into her, if you can."

Mr. Horn considered. Then, "Gabriella, it would seem to me that your mother made the decision for you a long time ago."

"She made it?"

"When she took you away from Cornell House. When she broke all ties with the family from which your father came."

"Why did she?"

He didn't answer me. His velvety eyes seemed suddenly less soft. They touched me, then shifted away to regard the blue of the sky.

William said, "Your mother had her reasons, wouldn't you say? And wouldn't you say they were good ones if she stuck to them?"

"She didn't want to live there without my father," I said.

But I knew that wasn't the whole truth. She had been frightened of something, of someone. She had run away.

I straightened up. I asked, "What was she scared of?"

William and Mr. Horn exchanged glances.

Then Mr. Horn said, "Perhaps she wasn't afraid. Perhaps she simply wanted to live elsewhere, wanted you to live elsewhere."

William said quietly, "Tell him about this morning, Gaby."

I hesitated. Then, "I fell off a horse. Don't make more of it than it is."

William's silver eyes met mine. I felt ashamed of myself. But I couldn't let myself trust him. I couldn't admit that I was sure someone had tried to kill me.

"You fell off a horse," Mr. Horn said softly. "Just like your father."

I shivered. I got to my feet. "I feel as if you are both against me, against Benjamin."

"No, you mustn't think that," Mr. Horn said softly. "I am for you, Gabriella. For you. Oh, yes, indeed." He looked as if he were about to say more. I saw a softening in his lips, his eyes.

Then William said, "I think we've talked quite enough."

Mr. Horn remained silent.

I knew that William was responsible. William hadn't really wanted to bring me here. He had probably fixed the car so it wouldn't run, just to keep me from coming, and now he had kept Mr. Horn from speaking to me freely.

Finally Mr. Horn said, "Gabriella, is it right, what you told me? You've come back only because of your planned marriage to Benjamin?"

"Of course. I'd have no other reason."

"Your mother. . . ."

"Mr. Horn," William said urgently.

The older man paused, thought, murmured, "Yes, yes, of course. But we must see to the lawyers, William."

"What lawyers?" I demanded.

He smiled at me, smoothed his circlet of white hair, and blinked. "Forgive me, an old man's wandering."

William cut in, "Gaby, what you should do, and I'm sure that Mr. Horn will agree with me, is to leave Cornell House right away."

I thought of what had happened that morning, my fall and the mists of death swirling around me. I thought of what I had begun to suspect. I would have wanted to do as William advised me. But I couldn't. I had to know the truth. I had to know who my enemy was. I had to learn what had happened

to my father, and why my mother ran away. I had
to prove my love for Benjamin.

I said steadily, "What do you have against me,
William?"

His big hands bunched up on his knees. He got up,
took a step toward me. I had the feeling that he
might grab me and shake me.

"Why, Gabriella," Mr. Horn said quietly, "Where
did you get such an extraordinary idea? What would
William have against you, my dear? Has Benjamin
been putting things into your small, beautiful head?"

"Benjamin never said. . . ." My voice trailed away.
In fact, I was remembering, Benjamin had had quite
a bit to say about William.

Mr. Horn went on, "And William is quite right,
you know. You must leave Cornell House. Now.
Today. Return to the city. Perhaps, within a few
months, you and Benjamin could be quietly married.
If, after a decent interval of courting, you decide that
you want to be."

William made an angry sound.

I rose, said quietly, "I don't understand this. I
don't think I want to." I turned to William, "Will you
please drive me back now, or shall I call Benjamin
and ask him to come for me?"

"I'll drive you," William said harshly. "But I don't
want to."

Mr. Horn walked with us to the car. He patted my
hand. "Bewildering, I know. Annoying in the ex-
treme. You feel that we are impertinent, if not worse.
Forgive us, Gabriella. We are concerned for you. In
the absence of facts, could you not try trusting us?"

I sensed the quick, hard honesty in him. I knew
that my father had trusted him. Yet I couldn't do
what he asked of me. I was committed now, and I

couldn't ever turn back. The dream was over. I had to face life as it came to me.

For most of the trip a heavy silence lay over William and me. I was satisfied to leave it that way. But he said, as we reached the mountain crest, and began the long ride down, "Mr. Horn is a good man. I don't expect you to trust me. But what about him?"

"I'm in love with Benjamin," I said quietly, as much to myself as to William. "I'm in love with him, and I'm going to marry him."

The storm came in slowly, with distant lightning and great long drum rolls of far off thunder. But by the time the evening was over, and I had gone to my bedroom, it had reached the wide terraces. Wind sucked at the casements of the house, and great white streaks of light spun across the meadows, while explosive thunder echoed back from the jagged teeth of the coastal cliffs.

For a long time, I stood at the window, peering through the rain spotted glass at the wild display. It was intense, frightening, yet I was fascinated by the sight and feel of untamed nature roaring so freely around me.

Finally I went to bed. I slept restlessly, dozing, then jolting awake, troubled by dreams I couldn't remember, wasn't sure that I wanted to remember.

Once, listening to the wind, I thought I heard footsteps, the rustle of clothing, the sound of the small cage elevator moving. I thought I heard those sounds, and strained to hear more but heard nothing. Surely Fernetta was not up and about at that time. Moments later, a door slammed. That time I was sure. I looked at my wristwatch. It was five o'clock.

The storm had abated. Now gentle rain fell on the roof. I soon fell asleep again.

By morning I rose, tired and heavy eyed. I dressed quickly in pants and shirt. I put on sneakers and hurried downstairs.

Bernard leaned crumpled against the stairway bannister.

Sally was with him, pale, wringing her hands, her dark circled eyes full of anguish.

"But where is she then?" Bernard demanded. "Have you searched the house?"

Through dry lips, I asked, "What's wrong?"

"Fernetta's gone," Sally cried. "I can't find her. She's gone, and the chair, and I don't even know where to look."

I didn't say anything.

I remembered the sounds I had heard in the night. With sinking heart I went outside, stared along the terraces.

William found me there.

He was pale, tight lipped.

We searched the terraces one by one.

We roused the Haleys, and they rode out to check through the meadows, through the pine stands.

William and I began a slow pacing off of the cliffs.

We were together when we saw the narrow tire tracks. We were together when we finally sighted Fernetta. She lay crumpled at the foot of where Lovers Leap had once been. The broken remains of her wheelchair were scattered on the rocks around her.

9

"RUN BACK TO the cottage," William said. "I'm going to climb down. I want to have a look at her." He sat down, edged himself cautiously to the rim, then turned, reaching for a foothold.

I followed him.

He raised silvery eyes, ordered, "Get Terrell, I tell you. Have him call for help."

But we both knew there was no help now for Fernetta, and what had to be done could wait.

I went after him, not answering, saving my breath for the long slow climb from rock to rock.

At last we reached the debris strewn beach.

Fernetta lay on her back, a green bloodied robe spread around her. Empty blue eyes stared at the empty blue sky.

William knelt beside her.

I thought of the sound of the elevator whirring in the night, the rustle of clothing, the footsteps. I thought of the closing of the downstairs door. "I think I heard her go out," I whispered through dry lips.

"What do you mean?"

I told him how I had awakened, what I had heard.

It seemed to me that the pallor deepened in his square face. His lips seemed rimmed in white. But he said only, "You couldn't have known, Gaby."

He drew me close, turned my face from the still body.

"If only I'd gotten up. . . ." I moaned into his chest.

Lovers Leap . . . her wide open blue eyes anxiously following every move that Benjamin made. Her petulant voice pleading for his attention, her blooming under his gentle voice. Her warning to me, her pleas that I go away. . . .

Lovers Leap. . . .

My heart ached for her, for what I had done to her. I said tiredly, "I should never have come back. I should never have met Benjamin. If I hadn't, Fernetta would still be alive."

Those were true words, but I didn't know how completely true they were then.

We covered Fernetta's body with William's shirt, and made the long hard climb up the cliff together. We hurried to the cottage.

The Haleys were terribly shocked at the news. Johanna collapsed and had to be put to bed. Terrell was gray and silent. Benjamin grimly used the phone to summon help.

William and I went up to the house to break the awful news to Sally and Bernard.

Helen was waiting on the terrace. She studied our faces anxiously, whispered, "It's bad news, isn't it?"

At William's nod, her blue eyes filled with tears.

She took me into her arms, held me close. "I'm sorry, love." Then she looked at William. "They're inside. I think they know, sense it. It's like when she was crippled. They're sitting together, staring at the wall."

William said he would see them alone, but I had to go with him.

It was just as Helen had said. Sally and Bernard sat together in the bright sunlight of the morning room, dead and gray faces turned toward the door.

William told them briefly what happened.

Sally screamed, buried her face in her hands, and Bernard seemed to shrivel before my eyes. "It wasn't supposed to happen," he groaned. "Oh, no, no, never this."

I thought of the purr of the elevator, the rustle of clothes, the closing of the downstairs door.

Two days later, Fernetta was buried in a small, private ceremony attended only by the family. Her death had been attributed to suicide while of unsound mind. The others seemed to accept that.

Bernard and Sally had seemed to shrink into silent and palefaced ghosts who withdrew from the sight of me, offering wordless reproach.

Helen put it into words. She had come into my room in her usual flyaway manner. She sank heavily into the rocker near the big window. She rubbed her red rimmed eyes and sighed, "There's been enough trouble in this house."

I nodded silently.

"Ten years of trouble," she went on. "Your father's death. Your mother's going away. Fernetta's accident. The way they all changed. And then, then when you came back, that almost terrible accident you had. Now Fernetta...."

She had summed it up so neatly. I had done the same through two sleepless nights. I was sure now that I saw a pattern. Not a pattern really, but bits and pieces of a puzzle that could fit together if only I knew how to do it, if only I had a few more bits to work with.

She went on, "You can stop it, Gaby. If you hadn't returned, Fernetta would still be alive. You must go. For her sake. For what she tried to do for you."

"Tried to do for me?"

"She was frightened when Benjamin brought you back."

"She loved him," I cried. "I can't blame her for that."

"She did," Helen agreed. "But she was frightened, too. That's why she called William."

"Fernetta called William?" I demanded, my voice shrill with disbelief. "But why?"

"I don't know why. I only know that's what she did."

"To somehow break up my engagement to Benjamin," I said. "And when she saw she couldn't do that...."

My words trailed off. It was no use. I wanted to convince myself that I wasn't to blame for Fernetta's death. But I knew I was. It was my fault if she had committed suicide. It was my fault if she had been ... I felt a ripple of resistance against the word. I froze, trying not to accept it. But, at last, it was there in my mind. Murder. Fernetta had been murdered because of me.

"Helen," I said, "oh, Helen. I didn't want her to die."

"I know that. She didn't want you to die either."

Later that afternoon, Benjamin took me for a stroll on the lower terrace. He smiled his tilted smile, his dark eyes warm with love. "You look drawn, Gaby. The atmosphere of the place is beginning to get to you."

"I keep thinking about Fernetta."

"I know, darling. But you must forget the past. Fernetta did what she had to do. No one could have stopped her. You must look forward to the future with me." His voice deepened. "Gaby, let's get married now. There's no need and no reason to wait. We can drive into the city today. We belong together. We mustn't allow the family, allow matters outside ourselves, to run our lives for us."

A cold shiver touched me. It was too soon. I could still see Fernetta's empty eyes. I told Benjamin how I felt.

He said quietly, "I know that, too, darling. But it will make everyone feel better. We'll have joy again in Cornell House."

Later I supposed that I allowed him to persuade me because, in my heart, it was what I wanted. I hoped that all my fears would be resolved when I became Benjamin's bride.

Then, without trying to understand, I agreed. "All right. Let's go to the city now."

He hugged me. "We'll be so happy together, darling. You'll see. Trust me. And everything will be the way Drago promised."

Drago, the gypsy. I remembered when she had promised me love, and I had already looked across the room into Benjamin's dark eyes, and found my love there. I had drifted in a dream of faith and trust, waiting expectantly for the miracle of joy to mantle me. Now, only a few weeks later, I had changed. I had felt the mists of death swirl around me. . . .

Benjamin didn't know those thoughts. He started to lead me toward the parking area.

I hung back, said, "I can't be married in a pants suit. I want to change. I want to comb my hair."

"Women!" he smiled. "Nobody will be there but us."

"We're the important ones," I insisted. "It won't take me long."

"I don't want anything to stop us, Gaby."

"Nothing will," I promised him.

But it was with a feeling of dread, rather than joy, that I hurried upstairs. I showered, made up. I brushed my hair into a cap of curls. I stood in briefs and bra, trying to decide between a short blue shift with a high collar and no sleeves and a white suit with a demure neckline. The white, I finally decided, looked more bride-like.

It was then that I began to falter. I didn't feel like a bride preparing for her wedding. I felt . . . it was hard to know just what I felt. But it was wrong. Wrong.

I had to force myself to slip into the white suit. I drew on my shoes, took up my dress. Though I knew Benjamin was waiting for me, I carefully hung away the clothes I had just taken off.

Helen met me on the stairs. She blocked the way, stared me up and down. "Where are you going, love?"

"Benjamin and I are driving into the city."

"What for?"

I swallowed. My throat was suddenly tight. I felt a flush rise in my cheeks. "We're going to be married today," I whispered finally.

"Married!" Helen gave me a single look, then turned and trotted down the steps, hurrying away to disappear into the shadows of the lower hallway.

I followed her more slowly, hurt and confused.

Helen had not wished me luck. Helen hadn't smiled. Helen hadn't kissed me and called me "love." She had plainly been more outraged—or had it been frightened, I wondered—than joyful.

My faltering resolve stiffened. I would show them. I would show them all. Benjamin and I would be married, and there was nothing anyone could do to stop it. But why were they all so against me? Why had they always been, from the moment I returned to Cornell House with Benjamin, so against me?

Bernard stood in the morning room doorway. He stared at me, reached out a shaking hand to hold me as I started by.

I saw the despair in his eyes. But more, something more. The shadows of terror darkened them.

From within, Sally cried, "No, Bernard, no. Come here, Bernard. Please come here."

As he stumbled away, the big front door opened. Benjamin stood on the threshold. "Ready?"

I went to meet him. Now he wore an azure blue jacket and paler blue trousers. His dark hair was brushed and shining across his forehead. "You're lovely," he said.

I hesitated for just a moment. I had an odd feeling that I was being hurried, rushed into something for which I was not quite prepared. Then I smiled back at him.

"Yes, Benjamin. I'm ready."

We were about to get into the car when William came walking down the path. His square face was flushed. His sandy hair was touseled. He was breathing hard. He said, "Look at the both of you. All dressed up. Is it for our benefit? Or are you planning to go somewhere?"

I had the feeling that he had raced down the hill, jumped from terrace to terrace trying to intercept us. I remembered how Helen had turned, left me on the stairway alone and disappeared into the lower hallway. Helen must have gone directly to William, gone to tell him what I had said. Helen had told me that Fernetta had called William to come to Cornell House. To come and stop me from marrying Benjamin. Now that was what William was trying to do. To keep his faith with her, I thought suddenly.

Benjamin grinned, "Gaby needs a break. We decided to dress up and go down to the Red Hen on the highway for a couple of drinks and a late lunch."

William's narrowed silver eyes gleamed at me, then glanced at the car. I knew he was certain of what we planned. I realized he was wishing the car wouldn't start. It reminded me of the day he had taken me to see Joshua Horn. Something had been wrong with the car then, and I had suspected that William, someone, had tampered with it. Now I wondered why. I had forgotten most of the conversation I had had with the old man in the excitement of Fernetta's death. But I knew there had been something he seemed to want to tell me, and was prevented from doing it by William, I thought. He was so insistent at first that I had returned for some reason other than to marry Benjamin. He had said something about calling the lawyers. It was all linked to my twenty-first birthday, now only ten days away. These were more pieces to fall into the pattern. . . .

William said, "You're not going out for drinks and

a late lunch. You're going to get married. Gaby looks like a bride, and like nothing but a bride."

"All right," Benjamin conceded, grinning. "But it's none of your business, is it?"

"I guess not. But why the lie?"

I didn't understand that myself. I didn't like it.

He shrugged, "I thought we might be able to avoid a lengthy discussion."

"But discussion is necessary," William answered.

"I think not."

"Fernetta." William paused. "Benjamin, she's hardly cold in her grave. You can't just pretend that nothing happened. It did happen."

"It's not our fault," Benjamin said coldly.

William was silent for a moment, then, "No one accuses you."

There was something ugly in the brief silence that followed. Then Benjamin opened the car door. "Get in, Gaby," he told me.

But I couldn't. I said, "Benjamin, it does seem. . . ."

"Abrupt, yes," William agreed. "It'll hurt Sally and Bernard terribly, and the way they already are. . . ."

"Regrettable," Benjamin said. "But we've waited long enough."

"You've hardly waited at all," William cut in. He looked at me. I suddenly remembered how he had held me when we had stood beside Fernetta's body. I felt the strength of his chest as I leaned against him. He said, "Gaby, do you really want to be married this way? Without your friends and family around you? To sneak off, as if what you're doing is something shameful?"

Benjamin's fingers tightened around my arm. He said, "That's ridiculous, William."

But I stopped him. I said, "No, Benjamin. No. I can't. William's right. We can't start out like this. And this *is* the wrong time. A few days more won't matter."

"Exactly," William agreed in his deep slow voice. "Just give Sally and Bernard a few days more in which to pull themselves together. Give them a chance to calm down."

Benjamin looked as if he were going to argue. There was a flush on his lean cheeks, and his dark brows were drawn in a frown.

"We have to," I told Benjamin. "It must be right."

A load seemed to slip from my shoulders. I knew now that I was making the best decision, the decision that I had wanted to make all along. A few days more surely wouldn't matter. I smiled up at Benjamin.

William stepped aside. "You won't be sorry," he told me. He turned, strode up the path. Moments later, he reappeared on the upper terrace. From there, I saw, he stood, looking down on us.

Benjamin saw him, too, and put my own thought into words. "Do you suppose that he's just making sure that I don't change your mind again?"

"I don't know," I answered thoughtfully.

Why had Fernetta been so opposed to my marriage to Benjamin that she called William to come to Cornell House? Had it been jealousy? Had it been fear? What could she have feared about my becoming Benjamin's bride?

Why was Helen so determined to stop me?

Why had Joshua Horn been so disapproving?

What could there be about Benjamin that made them all urge me to wait, urge me to go away? Or was it Benjamin? Was it me, myself?

Benjamin was saying, "I know what it is, Gaby." His voice was thin, silky, suddenly reminding me of Terrell.

I didn't ask him what. I didn't want to know. I had a sudden foreboding, a sense of discomfort.

But Benjamin went on, "He's in love with you." And smiling, "It's always been that way between us. He has it in for me. And he wants what I have."

"William? Oh, no, Benjamin, he's not in love with me. If anything he dislikes me."

Benjamin laughed. "Of course not. He's jealous. He wants you for himself." Benjamin bent his head close to mine. "And I'll tell you, Gaby, I begin to wonder now just how you feel about him."

I had my own sense of uncertainty to contend with. For a moment I remembered the touch of William's hand, his slow steady voice. But then I remembered that I had fallen in love with Benjamin the first moment that I saw him. It was Benjamin whom I loved.

I gave a shaky laugh. "Benjamin, you know how I feel."

"When he tells you no, then you agree," Benjamin pointed out. "That must mean something."

"Only that what he said made sense to me in this."

"But it made no sense to me. I want us to be married. Today. Today, Gaby. I don't see why we should guide ourselves by anything William Tysson says. He's an outsider, and has nothing to do with us. And. . . ."

"But he's right," I said firmly.

"No," Benjamin insisted. "He's just putting obstacles in the way. You'll see. In a few days, he'll think of some other reason why we should wait.

And after that he'll think of a few more. He's trying to break us up. Don't let him do it, Gaby."

"But why should he want to?" I demanded, voicing my innermost bewilderment.

"I told you. Because he wants you for himself maybe."

"No," I protested. "Not that. You can forget that."

"All right. I'll try to forget that. But suppose it's because of Fernetta. Because she killed herself. Because. . . ."

I felt my eyes sting with tears. "That's a good reason, Benjamin."

"No," he insisted. Then, laughing softly, "If I had any sense I'd grab you, put you in the car, drive you away from here. I'd marry you whether you call it the right time or not. I'd make you marry me, and then it would all be over."

"I can't help how I feel," I said softly.

"You'd be glad if I did it that way."

"I wouldn't. That's not how I picture my wedding, Benjamin."

"And a forced marriage isn't valid anyway." He paused. Then, laughing softly said, "But don't you know that the only reason I don't just carry you off is that I realize how you feel?" He drew a deep breath. When he went on his voice was husky, "But Gaby, don't you remember how it was? Don't you remember that night we met again? It was love the minute we looked at each other across the room. It was just as Drago told you it would be. We have to go back to that time, to recapture it, if we're to be to each other what we were meant to be."

When we met again . . . The fragments of that sentence blazed in my mind. I remembered Joshua Horn, at least I thought it was Joshua, telling me that the Haleys had come to Cornell House just two weeks before my father was killed, before my mother ran away with me. Benjamin always had implied that we had known each other when we were children, had grown up together. Yet I had scarcely remembered him as more than a vague, tall form standing beside his father.

It had all begun then. When the Haleys brought Bernard back from Las Vegas. My father's death. My mother's flight. Fernetta's crippling accident. Sally's descent into drinking. Bernard's wilting away. Then my return to a cold suspicious, fearful welcome. The hands of death reaching for me when I was thrown from Nellie's broad back, and the rusty nail I'd found. Fernetta's terrible end. The elevator, the footsteps and rustle of clothes. And Fernetta couldn't walk. So someone had been with her. She had been murdered. An attempt had been made to murder me. The picture was filling in. The misty image of threat was becoming more clear. But what had it to do with Benjamin? What?

His warm hands cupped my cheeks. He turned my face up, dark eyes staring intently into mine. "What is it, Gaby? What are you thinking?"

It was a time when I had to dissemble. I didn't know why. I wanted to trust Benjamin, but I couldn't tell him about my terrible thoughts.

"Don't you remember that night?" he went on.

"I do, Benjamin," I said softly. "And it will be that way again."

"Will it?" he asked bitterly. "Will you let it, Gaby? Or will you spoil it? Will you destroy everything, everything I want, you want, for the both of us?"

10

I DECIDED THAT I had to go back to see Joshua Horn.
But I didn't want to go through the charade of
asking Benjamin to take me, only to hear his excuses. I knew the same thing would happen if I were
to ask William. Besides, it was William himself who
had kept the old man from speaking freely to me before.

I tried to phone for a taxi. The operator, chuckling,
said, "Honey, we don't have taxis around here. If
you want one you'd better go to the city."

The feeling that I was a prisoner was stronger
than ever. I considered writing to Jessie, but I didn't.
Jessie probably thought Benjamin and I were
married by now. It would require more explanation
than I had patience for to tell her everything that had
happened.

Disconsolate and disturbed, I left the morning
room and went out on the terrace.

Bernard was standing at the stone balustrade looking off toward where Lovers Leap had once been, toward where Fernetta had died.

He gave me a brief glance from shadowed, filled eyes, then looked away. After a brief moment, he said, "It wasn't supposed to happen. If you hadn't come back...."

"What do you mean?"

His lips twisted. I saw the scar on his forehead redden. He seemed about to speak. Then Sally came out of the house. She staggered toward us, crying, "Bernard, no, come in here, Bernard."

He nodded, whispered, "I wash my hands of it, Gabriella."

The two of them went inside.

Hands clenched to keep them from trembling. I stood alone and considered. Bernard was terrified. So was Sally. But of what? More than ever I wanted to talk to Joshua Horn.

I wandered down to the cottage, hoping to distract myself by spending some time with Benjamin.

As I mounted the steps I heard his voice—low, hard, angry. "My way," he said.

"The stakes are too high," Terrell retorted.

"My way. So leave it alone," Benjamin answered.

The exchange didn't make sense to me, but it was somehow frightening. I backed down the steps and went to the corral.

Benjamin came out a few minutes later. He smiled, asked how long I'd been there. I told him I'd just come down.

"Joshua Horn was here a few minutes ago. I told him you were sleeping."

"But why did you do that?" I demanded. "I wasn't asleep, Benjamin. And I wanted to talk to him."

"You did?" Benjamin laughed. "Then I beg your pardon, Gaby. I thought I was saving you the boredom of a long visit with a dull old man."

But I saw the sharp look in Benjamin's eyes. I softened my tone. I said, "He's not so boring. I rather like him."

Benjamin ignored that. He said, "I'm going to saddle up Nellie for you, and Devil's Dancer for me, and we're going to take a ride. My mother's fixing up a picnic lunch. It's a good day for something like that."

"I don't think so, Benjamin."

"You're okay. You just had a small fall. There's no reason for you to be so wary about going again."

"I feel wary," I said.

"Ridiculous. If you don't try now, you'll probably never ride again," he argued.

"That will suit me fine," I retorted, thinking about the nail I'd found under Nellie's saddle blanket, about the terrible spin through the air that I'd experienced.

He muttered something that I didn't understand. I had noticed the sun glint on a car high on the crest of the mountainside. I watched it creep over, then down the curving dirt road.

Benjamin watched it, too, then acknowledged it, saying, "I think that's old man Horn on his way back. He doesn't believe in taking a 'no' for an answer."

I didn't answer him.

The stakes are too high, Terrell had said.

My way. So leave it alone, Benjamin had answered.

What was Benjamin's way? What were the stakes? I hurried to the parking area to meet Joshua Horn. He pulled in, stopped. He didn't get out.

"I'm sorry I missed you before," I told him.

He smiled, looked at Benjamin who had trailed along after me, and said, "I told Benjamin I'd be back. So here I am. Hop in and I'll take you for a ride."

Benjamin cut in. "We're going on a picnic."

I said, "We can do that any time, Benjamin."

He gave me a stony look.

I told Joshua that I'd run up and get a sweater and be right back. He said I mustn't hurry. He had plenty of time to spend waiting for a pretty girl.

Benjamin went up to the house with me, his face glowering disapproval. I tried to lighten his mood.

"Surely you're not jealous of Joshua Horn," I teased.

"In a way I am," Benjamin retorted. "I prefer that you spend your time with me, Gaby."

"But I do. I'll only be gone a few hours, if that."

"Will you? Or will you decide that you don't want to come back?"

"Benjamin!"

"Gaby, Gaby. . . ." he shook his head. "What's happening to us?"

"You know. . . ."

"But I don't know," he said. "You're stalling. I don't understand why. You let William talk you out of marrying me a few days ago. You've carefully not made any mention of it since. What should I think? What should I believe?"

"You might try trusting me a little," I told him, and ran up the steps.

When I came down, he was gone.

I hurried out to the parking area, got into the car with Joshua.

"I hope I haven't made trouble for you," he told me. His velvety eyes seemed worried. "You know that's the last thing I intend to do. William warned me, and even so I managed to say too much the last time, but since Fernetta's death. . . ."

"Benjamin's not exactly pleased," I confessed. "But I'm glad you came. I've been anxious to see you. I just couldn't seem to manage it, though."

"You wanted to see me?" he asked. He put the car into motion.

I nodded.

"Is it anything . . . anything special?"

"I'm not sure," I told him.

"But serious?"

"Yes."

"And you wanted to talk away from this place."

"Yes," I repeated.

He was silent then. He drove down the road slowly, following the sharp curves. He kept his white ringed bald head turned firmly toward the windshield, watching carefully.

"There's a small place, the Red Hen, just a few miles away on the highway. We'll stop there."

"I'd like to. Benjamin mentioned it once, but I've never been there."

It didn't take us very long. He pulled up, stopped in front of a small wooden building set in a grove of trees. The roof was red, the broad front porch walled in glass stripped with dark brown wood. It was pleasant inside, dark walls covered with huge copper platters, and big copper bowls filled with eucalyptus limbs.

Joshua ordered coffee for the both of us from a tall, bearded boy whose blue eyes seemed filled with worldly knowledge.

He sat opposite me, his wrinkled face expectant.

I tried to marshal my thoughts, my suspicions.

I had seen a pattern, before, to everything that happened at Cornell House beginning with my father's death. But now, looking into Joshua's eyes, I couldn't put it into words—remembering the brief exchange I overheard between Benjamin and Terrell, I didn't dare put it into words.

Joshua gave the returned waiter a brief smile as we were served. When we were alone again, he said, "You're very troubled, Gabriella. You're . . . I venture to say that you're frightened."

"Frightened," I repeated tonelessly.

"You have cause to be."

"What cause?" I asked.

"Fernetta's death was a terrible thing," Joshua said quietly. "Surely you've wondered about that."

I couldn't answer him. I couldn't speak of it. I didn't want to think of it any more.

"Do you think it really was suicide?" he asked gently.

I took a deep breath. I wanted to say, *Yes, yes, it must have been.* I didn't want to tell him the truth. But I couldn't hold back. I whispered, "No, I don't believe it."

"And why is that? Why should you suppose that she would go riding in her wheelchair near that terrible place in the middle of the night?"

My voice shook as I said, "I don't think she did. She was murdered. She wanted to save me. She wanted to help me. And that's why she was murdered."

His velvety eyes were suddenly obsidian hard. "That's a strong accusation, Gabriella."

"I heard sounds that night, Mr. Horn. I heard the elevator moving. I heard the rustle of clothing.

And most of all I heard footsteps. Fernetta couldn't walk. So someone was with her. Someone. . . ."

"But why should she allow anyone to take her out. . . ."

I was quiet for a long moment. I considered that for the first time. The answer seemed so simple once I thought of it. "She might have been drugged. Asleep. She might never even have known what was happening."

"So many things," he mused. "Your father . . . your mother running away. . . ."

I waited breathlessly.

He finished his coffee in a long gulp. I had the feeling that he had made up his mind about something. He said, "Gabriella, in the name of your father and mother, I ask you, I beg you, I plead with you to go away from that place. Now. Today. I beg you to let me take you into the city. And to never return to Cornell House."

I stared at him. "But why?"

"I've told you. You're in danger there."

I knew that. I had felt death reaching for me. But I didn't understand. I had to know why, what the threat was.

I asked, "Won't you explain?"

"I'm not sure that I have any explanation, Gabriella. I can't tell you what I don't know myself. But I can tell you what I do know. Your return was a mistake. You must accept that. You must leave."

"But Benjamin. . . ."

"You must leave Benjamin, too."

I stared at Joshua. "Do you mean that Benjamin might . . . might. . . ."

"I do not mean to implicate Benjamin, nor anyone else. I say only. . . ."

"I can't leave," I said.

"But why not, child? Why are you tied there? If your mother could run away as she did, then surely you, as young as you are, can make a new life. . . ."

"I am going to marry Benjamin."

"Is that wise?"

"Did William tell you to ask me that?" I demanded.

Joshua smiled faintly. "William? William has warned me to say nothing to you."

"Say nothing? Nothing about what?"

Joshua shrugged.

"William is against the marriage, too," I said slowly.

"Gabriella, don't waste your precious time and strength on foolish speculations. Simply go away."

I sat very still, my hands folded in my lap.

"The thing to consider is your own life, safety. Do you see?"

I didn't answer him.

"It began so long ago, we may never know the truth of it."

"What began?"

"This . . . this tragedy," he told me.

"With my father," I said. "I've realized that much. He was murdered, wasn't he?"

Joshua's wrinkled face was carved into pale stone. He didn't answer me.

"You mentioned lawyers," I reminded him.

He sighed, "Gabriella, I can say nothing now, but this one thing. You must go away."

"I can't." I looked at the solitaire that gleamed on my finger. It wasn't just a bauble, a meaningless jewel. It was a symbol of trust, of love. I had to know the truth.

Aloud, I said, "I'll find out what happened, Joshua. But it won't be from the city. It will be in Cornell House itself."

I was dressing for dinner. I zipped my pink shift, and stepped into pink sandals. My mind was still on my meeting with Joshua Horn.

The door behind me suddenly flew open. In the mirror, I saw a gleam of red hair, a three-cornered grin.

"Jessie!" I cried, hurrying to meet her.

"In the flesh," she laughed. "And don't faint. Why, Gaby, you've suddenly gone pale."

"Where on earth did you come from? How did you happen to? How long can you stay?"

Jessie sauntered into the room. Her pants suit was apple green. Her thick heeled shoes were made of golden straps. She dropped a gold purse on the bed. "One thing at a time, and one question at a time, Gaby." She curled into the rocking chair, drawing her long legs under her, her smile widening. "I thought you'd just about flip, and you really have, haven't you?"

"It was just that I've been so wanting to talk to you."

"You sound terribly serious, Gaby. Is something wrong?"

I hesitated. Then I said, "Not exactly."

"Not exactly," she repeated dryly. "That's not very explicit, is it?" She fluttered long, mascara darkened lashes at me. "It's nice to know you've been thinking about me. I was beginning to wonder. I did expect a note from you, a phone call. Something." Her husky, laughing voice had a note of re-proof in it.

I said, "Jessie, I'm sorry. It's just been ... well, it's been so hectic."

Jessie's smile grew less bright. The laughter was gone from her voice. She said, "Gaby, you know, I got to worrying about you. After all, I *did* introduce you to Benjamin. And I knew the minute I ran into him on the street and invited him that he'd be crazy for you and you for him. So I feel responsible. I don't like it, sweetie. But I *do* feel responsible. So you quit your job, and left with him, and I never heard a word. Not a single word. I mean, after all, I just expected to hear something. Maybe a postcard from your honeymoon. Well, anyway, something. When there was this big dead empty silence, I got ... to tell you the truth, Gaby, I got squeamish. And it was my vacation coming up. I told you I wouldn't be at work along about this time. So I just packed a bag, and came on down."

"I'm so glad that you did," I said fervently.

"I was so sure," she said, "I'd have sworn an oath, that you and Benjamin would have been married by now. I had the distinct impression that you didn't plan to wait any time at all before you. ..."

Her eyes were a clear, cold, unsmiling green. They made me feel that I was a germ trapped beneath a glass shield.

I said quietly, "Well, you know, a lot has happened, Jessie. Things don't always. ..."

"Things don't always what?"

I drew a deep breath. I said, "I'm afraid there's been some trouble here, Jessie. That's why we delayed."

"Trouble?" Jessie uncoiled her long legs and put

her gold sandals on the floor. She pushed, and the rocker snapped back and forward. "What are you talking about?"

I said faintly, "It's very complicated."

Jessie answered, "Listen, Gaby, I drove in a little while ago. I didn't know exactly where to stop, or what, so I parked the car near the others, and then walked around to the front. You know, where the terraces end. Who should come trotting out of that white square building but Benjamin. He briefed me a bit. That is, he told me how to find you up here, and that you were somehow holding back on getting married. So how about you stop beating around the bush and just explain?"

I grinned. "Trust you to put your finger on it right away," I told her. Then, "Jessie, tell me something, will you? Do you think Benjamin really loves me?"

Jessie looked at me blankly. Finally she examined her long bronze fingernails. After that she sighed. "Okay. You ask a silly question. You get a silly answer. Yes, I think Benjamin really loves you. Now what does that have to do with what?"

The stakes are too high, Terrell had said.

My way. So leave it alone, Benjamin had answered.

Leave Cornell House, Joshua Horn pleaded.

"Jessie, it's hard to explain," I said aloud. "I just didn't feel very welcome here when I came. And it threw me, I think."

"You're not the first girl to find that parents aren't too overjoyed to give up their only sons," Jessie said.

"Then Fernetta Tysson, my cousin, either . . . either committed suicide, or died accidentally, or. . . ." I didn't mention the third possibility. The one that I believed now to be the only explanation for Fernetta's death. I found that I couldn't speak of murder to Jessie.

"Okay," Jessie said. "And now what has that to do with you? With Benjamin?"

"She was in love with him," I said softly.

Jessie gave me a sympathetic look. "Oh, I see. But still, that's how things go, isn't it? Somebody wins. Somebody loses. What can you do? Except realize that you can't be responsible for what a poor crippled neurotic girl does."

"That's what Benjamin says, too, more or less."

"I should imagine so," Jessie said dryly.

I waited for a moment, then I asked, "Jessie, where did you meet Benjamin? I mean before that time on the street?"

She grinned, looked down at her nails. "Oh honestly, Gaby, you do have a terrible case of prenuptial willies. Which all girls go through. I'm here to stand by and assist in any way I can." She paused. Then, "You asked how I met Benjamin. The truth is, I'm not sure any more. It was ages and ages ago. Somebody's house. Then somebody else's. Then somebody else's again. I've known him long enough to know him. And then we met on the street, and the rest should be ancient history for you."

I let my breath out in a sigh, asked, "Jessie, can you stay for a while?"

"I hope to. That is, if I'm welcome. I think you need my moral support. I don't know what's bothering you and Benjamin, but if you need a shoulder to yell on, I'm available."

"I feel better already," I said, laughing.

"So do I," Jessie said. "Now that I've finally seen you."

Only later I remembered that I hadn't told her about Nellie and the nail under her blanket. I hadn't described Bernard's terror. I had skimmed over the truth of Fernetta's death. I hadn't told her about the warnings I'd received from Helen and Joshua and William. I hadn't put into words my terror.

And it was long after that before I realized that I had questioned her about her meeting with Benjamin. I had asked her about it, without even knowing what it was that I wanted to know.

We were on the terrace having our before dinner drinks. I had changed again, to a blue dress, full skirted, round necked. I forgot that it was my birthday party dress until Jessie gleefully pointed it out to me. Then, embarrassed somehow, I quickly changed the subject.

Sally, her thin face expressionless, her eyes ringed with dark bruises, suggested that Jessie might like to stay on with us for a while. I was relieved that I hadn't been forced to ask for permission.

Jessie promptly accepted, as though she had already made up her mind that she was going to remain, invited or not.

I noticed how William's eyes returned more and more often to Jessie. She was wearing a slim, black dress with a deep plunging neckline. Her red hair was burnished. Her green eyes shone.

I felt somewhat uneasy to see the look in William's silver eyes, but Jessie glowed under their examinations, and soon after dinner, she and William disappeared together on an exploring trip of the extensive grounds.

At bedtime, Jessie came into my room.

She placed herself on the coverlet, then threw herself at full length. "That's a lot of man, that William."

I nodded.

"Another cousin of yours, is he?"

"I guess so."

"You guess so? You mean you don't know? All these people around here, and you're not even sure who they are? Now take Terrell Haley ..."

"He's not actually family, Jess. It's Johanna that's the Tysson."

"Oh, all right. But you know what I mean. There's him. And Benjamin, and William ... I tell you a girl could lose her mind trying to choose which one, couldn't she?"

I saw that her green eyes were searching mine in question. "I have chosen," I said.

"Of course you have. Then why are you stalling? Benjamin could very possibly be snapped up by someone less uncertain, Gaby."

"Don't, Jessie," I protested.

"But it's true. Why don't you tell me what's going on?"

I wanted to, but I couldn't. Something prevented me from telling her what terror was in my heart, what fear there was in my mind. I said only, "I guess I don't know what is."

"So then, don't you remember what Drago told you?" Jessie asked curiously. "Didn't you care what she promised? And then he was there, right before you, waiting to be discovered."

"I remember. And I care," I said. "But I just. . . ." I let the words trail away. I didn't know how to explain my fear. I didn't know why I didn't want to.

Jessie grinned. "Okay. It's just what I told you. Prenuptial willies. We'll get you over that in no time."

But that was the night when new terror touched me, and the shadows thickened around me, and I was suddenly reminded how closely I lived with the danger of death.

11

I WAS DEEP in dreamless sleep. Then, suddenly awake, I was aware of the dark room, touched only by the faint glimmer of light at the window.

I sat up, knowing that there had been a faint noise somewhere nearby. An unidentifiable sound had penetrated my suspended consciousness. Unidentifiable now, but it had frightened me. I could feel my heart pounding against my ribs, and my breath come in quick, shallow pants.

I listened and heard nothing. I waited, straining to hear, for what seemed endless time but could only have been a minute or two. Then, just as I was about to dismiss the sound as imagined, I heard it again.

A faint click, a purr. The jostle of metal against metal. Fernetta's small elevator was in use again. In use for the first time since her death.

Who had touched the controls?

Who was stealthily riding in the small metal cage?

There are moments when fear paralyzes. There are others when fear is so strong a fuel that reaction cannot be denied.

I found myself slipping from my bed. I moved soundlessly across the thick carpet, and found my robe. I slipped into it and tied the belt firmly, armoring myself unconsciously, I supposed, for what was to come.

Someone was moving through Cornell House in the still hours with an evil intent I couldn't guess. I knew that I must learn the identity of that person.

I inched the door opened, listening again.

Then I was absolutely sure. Yes, the small elevator at the back of the long dark hallway was in movement again.

For just an instant, I hesitated. The shadows were pitch black. The dim bulb that should have lit the interior of the cage was not burning. But then, as if inexorably drawn, I went down through the darkness.

I moved in silence on the rug, but my robe rustled, reminding me of the sound I had heard on the night Fernetta died.

I felt my way, fingers lightly touching the wall, brushing the frames of the pictures. By then the whine and purr had stopped. The darkened cage was there, its barred door half ajar. I peered inside.

It was empty, I thought.

But some instinct must have warned me. Perhaps it was an unconsciously felt drawn breath. Perhaps it was an air current created by nearby movement. I suddenly dodged back. I hit something hard but yielding. I heard a gasp that might have been my own, or might have been another's. Then I felt a blow at my shoulders, a vicious thrusting blow, and fingers burning through the quilt of the robe to my shoulders. I was flung violently forward.

I fell into the cage, sprawling, and helpless. My head slammed into the bars and there was a moment of stunning pain, sprinkled with the blaze of lights skyrocketing through my vision. I couldn't move or cry out. I heard the barred door click shut. The elevator gave a purr and a rattle. It moved and jerked, and then, with a great shrill of tearing gears, it simply let go.

The cage slammed on its chains and bounced and fell.

I felt the floor fall away from me, and my body thrown this way and that until some heavy weight tipped on me, crushing me down, driving the breath from my lungs and high horrified screams from my throat.

Death seemed to reach upward with a big black hand.

Time seemed to stop.

The cage dropped, banging and rattling on its chains, shrilling on its holding wires.

Then, with a roar that was like an explosion, it slammed onto its concrete base.

Dying echoes faded, and were revived by the sound of running feet, of voices crying out incompleted questions.

The crystal chandelier of the lower hall suddenly bloomed with light, throwing dull dusty shadows along the walls.

I moaned, tried to move from beneath the weight that pinned me.

I heard William's voice, slow and deep as ever,

but urgent now. He said. "Don't move, Gaby. Let me get in there."

My shocked and pained body continued to struggle. I heard the bars rattle, the sound of his breath straining. I heard him swear. The bent bars of the door gave way as he wrenched them aside.

Then he was bending over me.

He lifted the weight from me and I could breathe again.

He rose up and turned and thrust something away from him.

Beyond him, I saw the others. Jessie was there, in an exotic lacy robe, of which I somehow took note, even then. Bernard was hunched against the wall, his eyes starting with terror. Sally sobbed harshly. Helen was a small explosion, thrusting herself among them.

William leaned over me again, silver eyes gleaming, his mouth grim and lined with white. His hands moved over me in quick inventory, gentle and reassuring, and I remembered the day Nellie had thrown me, and he had touched me thus. It had meant comfort then, and it meant comfort now. But I wondered if it were a false comfort. I asked myself if it had been he who had been behind me in the dark. He who had thrust me into the small cage to die. He who was now disappointed at my second miraculous escape.

In that confused and fearful moment, I knew no discretion, nor dissembling. I cried, "Somebody pushed me into the elevator. I heard a noise and came to see what it was. And somebody threw me into it, and then it fell. It was fixed to fall somehow, that's why it fell."

The incompleted questions were suddenly stilled.

Silence hung like a muffling blanket over the hall-way.

Five pairs of eyes stared at me, focused like one single beam to where I lay on the floor of the cage with William kneeling beside me.

I wished that I had held my tongue, kept my own counsel. Any one of them might have been that shadowy figure in the hallway behind me. Anyone of them might have run the small cage up and down, until I was awakened, and heard the noise, and was thus lured out to my dangerous rendezvous.

Jessie, her face white above black lace, cried, "Gaby, have you gone quite mad? What are you talking about? Why were you wandering around? What were you doing in that thing, with that crazy wheelchair, too?"

At first I didn't know what she was talking about. Then I realized that a wheelchair stood in the hall. William had pulled it off me, thrust it out there. It was Fernetta's spare wheelchair that had been in the cage with me.

I shuddered with a wave of revulsion that swept me from head to toe.

William stroked my shoulder, offering wordless consolation.

Helen's gray face was glistening with unchecked tears. "Oh, no," she sobbed. "Dear God, not again."

Sally demanded harshly, "Why did you have to come back?"

In a thick unrecognizable voice Bernard said, "She's in shock. You mustn't listen to her. She doesn't know what she's saying."

He was afraid. Now, tonight. He had been afraid, I realized, from the moment of my return. There was no time then to wonder why. I must think of

it later, I told myself. I must find out how I could
be a threat to my uncle.

Only William seemed to take me seriously. His
eyes narrowed. He leaned close, said in a whisper,
"Gaby, are you sure?"

"I know," I said. "I felt it. A blow at my shoulders.
Someone threw me into the elevator, and then set it
going, and then. . . ."

He slid his arms under me, drew me close to his
chest. I clung to him as if he were the last rock of
safety in a spinning world. And yet, terribly, I suspected that he might have been responsible. He had
come to Cornell House immediately after I arrived,
summoned by Fernetta according to Helen, whom
I believed. He had been there when I fell from
Nellie. And he had been here again tonight. I reminded myself that the same was true of all the
others. I had no real reason to accuse him in my
mind.

He made his way through the group, carrying me
easily, as if I were a child within his arms, as my
father had carried me so many years before.

But I was a child no longer. I was a woman faced
with the imminence of death.

He put me on the bed, sat down beside me.

He said quietly, "Gaby, I don't think you should
talk any more now. Just rest and catch your breath.
Let's make sure that you're all right."

I tried to control my trembling. I breathed slowly
and deeply, and lay very still, waiting for the fingers
of terror that still clasped me to relax their awful
grip.

At last, through fear dried lips, I said, "I'm not
really hurt, William. I was just . . . it was just so
terribly frightening."

"Yes," he said simply. "Yes, Gaby, I know."

I wondered what he was thinking. I wished that I could read his mind. Did he know that there had been an attack on me? Did he believe what I had said? Did he realize that his warnings had been proved to be true? Or did he, like the others, imagine that I had somehow gone into the elevator just when it had broken free of its moorings? Did he believe now that I had had another odd accident?

I remembered Nellie leaping away, the saddle slipping, the stirrups flying. I remember the ground moving beneath me, my body rolling and helpless under the threat of angry hooves. I felt myself sail through the air, landing with a breathtaking thud, and William's arms around me. I remembered the long sharp nail I had found under the saddle blanket and hidden away. . . .

And now, tonight. . . .

That was the second time that death had reached out for me.

Every moment that I spent in Cornell House was a moment of threat to me.

But why?

Why would anyone hate me so? What had I come home to with Benjamin?

It was as if the thought of him had conjured him from the distance.

Suddenly he came into the room, breathless, pale, disheveled. "Gaby! What's going on here?"

Johanna and Terrell were with him, equally disheveled and heavy eyed, as if just aroused from sleep.

Jessie drawled, "I'm afraid we've had a small accident, Benjamin. Poor Gaby got up and went into that funny little elevator." She paused. Her husky voice had some odd meaning to it when she went on, "Though I really can't think why she should do a thing like that in the middle of the night. Perhaps she was sleepwalking."

Benjamin gave her a quick, dark look. He brushed William's shoulder, urging him away, and when William rose and stepped back, took his place on the edge of the bed. He bent his head to me, "Gaby, darling. What is it? We saw all the lights. We couldn't imagine...."

The confusion and terror of just moments before were gone now. I wished I hadn't cried my accusations aloud, broadcast a warning. It was time to retreat and retract. In self-protection I knew I must do that.

I said, "It was nothing, Benjamin. I'm fine. You can see that I'm fine now, can't you?"

"She says," Bernard put in thickly, "that someone attacked her, threw her into the elevator, then made it drop. She says...."

"Attacked her?" Terrell's silky voice was more amused than alarmed. "But whatever for? Who'd do a thing like that?"

"It must have been the door that hit her," Johanna said quietly. "What else could it have been? That door always did have a hair trigger. Fernetta...." Her voice faltered. "Poor Fernetta often complained about it." She gave Bernard a straight look. "You remember that."

"Yes," he agreed. He sounded tired, bewildered. His eyes were still fearful and his scar burned red. "Yes. I guess she did. Several times. That door always did have a way of slamming to."

I smiled faintly, finding it easy now to pretend.

"I'm sorry. I guess I was so terribly frightened when it happened. I just. . . ."

"We all understand," Jessie cut in. She yawned broadly, then smiled her three-cornered smile.

Benjamin glanced up. "I think the rest of you might as well go back to bed. Gaby needs to rest."

William said, "I'll see you in the morning."

"Thank you," I told him. "For . . . for getting me out of there."

He left the room.

Helen wanted to bring me some brandy to steady me. I told her she didn't need to bother. I was all right now. I just wanted to go back to sleep.

Benjamin shepherded her out, the others with her.

Only he and Jessie remained with me.

She sat on one side of me, he on the other.

She said, "Gaby, what was all that about?"

"I don't know," I answered. "I feel so confused."

But I wasn't confused. What had happened to me that night was part of the pattern, another piece had fallen into place. My return to Cornell House had triggered someone's terror. It had to do with my father's death, my mother's flight. I had twice been attacked as a result of it. Fernetta had died as a result of it. She had tried to save me, and I had thought her jealous. Helen had warned me and I had thought her a nervous old woman. William had told me to leave and I had thought him a busybody, trying to help Fernetta. Joshua Horn had begged me to go, but by then I had been determined to know the truth. I was more determined than ever to collect those missing pieces of the puzzle that would show me the whole truth of what had happened in Cornell House.

I knew I mustn't allow my face to reflect that determination. I must convince Benjamin and Jessie, and all the others as soon as I could, that I suspected nothing. That I had been frightened and hysterical when I made those earlier accusations.

Jessie's green eyes gleamed amusement at me. She said, "I can understand your being confused. After all, when people go sleepwalking. . . ."

I was glad that I hadn't tried to persuade Jessie. I knew she was on my side, but I knew, too, that she would never believe me.

There were too many questions in Benjamin's dark eyes. He wouldn't have been able to believe me either.

He said quietly, "Darling, can't you tell me what's wrong? Why this hysteria? Why are you so distressed?"

I answered, "I'm so sorry, Benjamin. I didn't mean to make such a fuss. I feel like a terrible fool."

"But you do realize now what happened, don't you?" he asked. "You were wandering around in the dark, I suppose. And maybe you bumped into the elevator door and it snapped to and hit you, and then you fell and struck the wrong button."

"It hasn't been used for some time," Jessie said. "Maybe that's why it fell like that."

"I suppose so," I agreed. I turned my head away, closed my eyes. "I think I'd like to go back to sleep now."

"Go along," Jessie ordered Benjamin. "You can see she's okay, can't you? No need here for panic. I'll just tuck her in, and sit with her for a little while. I'll make sure she's sound asleep before I go back to bed."

I murmured a protest, but when Benjamin had

gone, Jessie turned off the overhead light, switched on a small bedside lamp, and sat down beside me. She smoothed the coverlet over my shoulder. "Listen, sweetie, why don't you tell old Jessie what this is really all about? What's troubling you anyway?"

"I don't know," I said tiredly.

"Of course you do." Jessie's voice was suddenly sharp. "You must. Why, ever since I got here, I've had the feeling. . . ." She paused. Then, "Why don't you want to talk about it?"

I *did* want to. That was the trouble. I yearned to tell her my terror. But I knew it was no use. She wouldn't believe me, or understand. That was what I thought then. But I think now that there was some small part of me that knew I must trust no one. No one at all.

She asked, "Gaby, are you in love with Benjamin?"

I glanced at the solitaire on my finger. Its brilliant facets sparkled. I nodded.

"Then what's all this stalling about? Why don't you get married tomorrow?"

"Another few days," I said.

"But why the delay?" she insisted. Then, "Listen, sweetie, you could be making a terrible mistake. Benjamin is very attractive, and obviously rich, and he adores you. But if you continue to behave so strangely, he might. . . ."

Obviously rich, Jessie had said. *Obviously rich.*

But he had referred to himself as a poor relation. I was sure I remembered that. Or had it been Terrell who had said it? Now I just wasn't sure.

A picture formed in my mind. We were at the corral. My parents. Me. Terrell, with Benjamin in the background. The horses were saddled. My father said something, and Terrell answered, "I might as well earn my keep." Soon after, my father had died.

A shiver touched me. Had Terrell been earning his keep all these years? It seemed to me suddenly that he, rather than Bernard, ran Cornell House. The pool for Johanna. The banishment of the dogs. Did such triviality have a meaning? And why was Bernard so afraid?

Jessie said now, "Sweetie, I'm so worried about you. I wish you'd let me help."

I shut my eyes. "I'm tired."

"You weren't serious, were you?" she insisted. "All that nonsense about somebody knocking you into the elevator? You made it up, didn't you? To explain your screaming and all that."

I whispered, "I was just mixed up."

She rose, leaned close, said, "Go to sleep, sweetie. You'll be okay tomorrow. It'll seem like a bad dream. Just remember that gypsy, Drago, and her promise. You've found Benjamin, and now there's a wonderful future in store for you."

Terrell and Benjamin had been busy boarding up the small elevator when I came down for breakfast.

When they had finished, it was closed off with plywood. It seemed that nothing was left of the night before but my concealed terror.

The elevator was gone now, just as Fernetta was gone now, as it had been intended that I, too, should be gone.

No one mentioned what had happened.

Except for the raw wood around the shaft, across the doors, it might have all been a bad dream through which I had suffered and screamed, but about which none of the others could guess.

Benjamin suggested that he saddle Nellie for me, and I try a ride.

I begged off, offering no excuse.

Terrell laughed silkily, "I believe, my dear, that you're allowing your fear to rule you."

William and Jessie came in together. They had been out for an early walk, they announced. It was a beautiful day.

Jessie's green eyes sparkled. Her smile glowed. She exuded excitement and happiness.

William's square strong face seemed relaxed and pleased.

Later, when Jessie and I were alone, Jessie said, "I'm so glad I came down to check up on you, Gaby."

"So am I," I told her.

"For selfish reasons," Jessie laughed. "Oh both sides, of course. You needed some moral support and here I am. I'm relieved that you're going to be okay. And I think you are, judging by how you look this morning. But also," her three-cornered smile flashed at me, "there's the matter of William. I have to confess . . . he's really quite a man, isn't he?"

I felt a peculiar tightening in my chest. I said cautiously, "I guess so. I can't say I know him very well."

"Nor do I," Jessie laughed. "But I hope to. I want to. And if I have my way, I centainly will. Besides, besides, we both know him as well as you knew Benjamin when you fell in love with him, don't we?"

I forced myself to return her smile. I said, "You're right, Jessie. And I wish you luck."

"I don't believe in luck," she answered. "Except insofar as I make it myself. That's what I think luck is. What you make for yourself." She might have said more, but Helen came in, rushing as always.

She looked sideways at Jessie, then told me, "Mr. Horn is on the phone. I told him you'd be right down to talk to him."

"Oh, Helen, tell that man, whoever he is, that she'll call him back some other time," Jessie said. "Gaby's just come upstairs to rest. She needs to take it easy after what happened last night."

But I had already gotten to my feet. It seemed to me that every time Joshua Horn tried to reach me someone stood in the way. I was tired of it. I was going to put a stop to it. I wouldn't allow myself to be imprisoned in Cornell House. I said sharply, "I want to talk to him, Helen. I'm coming right now."

12

JESSIE GAVE ME a startled look. "Excuse me, sweetie."
I didn't answer. I ran down the steps, and into the
morning room.

Joshua's voice, when I picked up the phone, said
hello, was soft and steady. "Gaby? Is that you?"

There seemed to be a hum on the line. I wondered
if he were having difficulty hearing me.

"Mr. Horn? Yes. It's me. Gaby. Thank you for
calling. I wanted to. . . ."

He broke in. "Gabriella, I'd like to drive over
and pick you up. Perhaps we could go for a short
drive this morning. Would that suit you?"

The words were measured, and stressed, fraught
with an unspoken meaning.

I said, "I'll be waiting for you."

"In half an hour then."

As I prepared to hang up, I heard a faint click.
Then I understood the hum on the line. Someone

had been listening on one of the several extension phones. I wondered who it was, and how I could identify the listener. There seemed to be no way.

I went back to my room.

It was empty now. Jessie had gone.

A big black album lay on my bed. Its leather cover was worn in spots, the binding frayed. The gold leaf trim was faded.

As I picked it up a wave of nostalgia swept me. It felt right in my hands, familiar and safe. I opened it, fully prepared. My mother's face looked out at me. Not as I remembered her in these last years, not lined and sickly. But young and beautiful, and full of the warm glow of happiness. My father stood with her, so tall and gay. The date, written in faded blue ink, was just about eleven years before. The picture must have been taken very shortly before my fathers's death, I realized. With a wrench of the heart, I took the album to the rocker. I sat down, slowly turning its leaves. There were pictures of Fernetta, small, smiling, dark haired, with the promise of real beauty. There were pictures of Sally and Bernard. How different they had been then. Sally, slender but curved, very fashionably dressed; Bernard, unscarred and debonair, with the hint of the bon vivant in his smiling eyes and curved mouth. There were no pictures at all of the Haleys. None of Johanna and Terrell. None of that young Benjamin that I seemed to remember so vaguely. But, of course, now I knew why. The Haleys had come to Cornell House just barely two weeks before my father's death, before my mother fled. A younger Joshua Horn was in some of the snapshots. A Helen who looked exactly as she did today. I sat on my father's shoulders in one. I clung to my mother's skirt in another. It was a beautiful and precious record of what had once been, of lives interrupted by the hand of fate. Why had my mother not taken it when the two of them left Cornell House, I asked myself. Was it because she couldn't bear the memories it had the power to evoke? Or was there another reason? Was it because she hadn't wanted me to remember Cornell House, remember Sally and Bernard and Fernetta?

Voices suddenly caught my attention. Silky and low, wordless, but somehow emphasized. That had to be Terrell. And Bernard, gruff, and angry, and frightened. Yes, that was what it sounded like. Bernard was frightened. He said, "Terrell, I can't take any more."

Terrell's silky voice murmured a reply. I could imagine him smiling.

Johanna said, "It's all your fault, Bernard. Yours. And from the very beginning. Just keep that in mind."

They were on the terrace below, I knew.

I felt a strange sense of having lived through these moments before. Lived through them, listening, straining, and not understanding. It had happened recently, just after I came back. But it had happened before then, too. Long long ago, when I was a child, made uneasy by loud tones and argument.

Bernard said, "I wash my hands of it. I tell you, I can't take any more. And I won't."

Terrell's murmur faded. There were footsteps, then silence.

The scene below was finished, I realized. I sank back, panting without knowing why. It seemed to me that a further threat had sifted into the room on the still air. A threat that I remembered from the past but could not quite identify. The album slipped from my lap.

A white rectangular card fell from its opened pages.

I thought it was another picture. I picked it up and turned it over. But it was not a picture. It was a business card. I stared at the neat black print. The Craddock Detective Agency. An address in the city. A city phone exchange.

I hurried to put it into my purse, hiding it without knowing.

Jessie knocked, then came in. She grinned, "It looks as if you're stuck with it. The old man is down there. He's impatiently waiting, but trying to be polite about it. Terrell is entertaining him, but not succeeding very well. I think the old man doesn't care much for Terrell. I can't think why. He's a very attractive man. Anyhow, you've still got a chance to make your excuses. But if you insist on a dull couple of hours, then you'd better hurry down before the old man has apoplexy on the front terrace."

I tucked my purse under my arm, went downstairs.

Jessie trailed me, saying, "It's a lovely day for a ride. I guess. I don't blame you after all. I wish I were going, too."

I understood the hint, but pretended not to. I agreed it was a nice day, and moved even more quickly.

"Maybe I can talk William into doing something," Jessie went on.

"A good idea," I answered, and stepped out onto the terrace.

Joshua Horn rose quickly from the white wrought

iron bench on which he had been waiting. He gave a small bow, a quick thin smile. He made polite goodbyes to Terrell and Johanna, to Jessie as well, and then swept me down to the car.

He wasted no time in talk until he had the car under way. Then he sighed, "I dislike this place nowadays. It has a stench that offends me." Then, with a shrug, "Never mind. Tell me, are you all right, Gabriella?"

I nodded. I wasn't sure what he knew, if he knew anything.

He said "Helen called me this morning quite early. She loves you, Gabriella. She was distraught to the point of making very little sense indeed. It took a great deal of questioning to determine what had happened last night in that accursed house."

I swallowed hard. I didn't want to talk about it. I didn't know if I could.

"Helen said that you claimed someone attacked you, that you later said you must be mistaken."

I nodded again.

"And which was the truth?"

I didn't answer him.

"Gabriella, you know that I have been concerned for you ever since your return to Cornell House. I have several times suggested that you must leave. Surely you realize that you can trust me?"

I didn't answer him.

He smiled faintly. "Wise child. You have learned a great deal in a short time, haven't you? Very well. We shall stop at the Red Hen. We shall have coffee and discuss this in an orderly fashion. I will tell you a number of facts that may be useful to you. I shall expect complete candor from you. Is it agreed?"

"Agreed," I murmured, my heart suddenly beating very hard.

I knew that I must trust someone. I must talk to someone. It could have been Jessie, of course. Jessie was my dear friend. Jessie was clever and quick. But . . . but something held me back. She might laugh at my suspicions. She might think me mad. Worse she might repeat them to Benjamin, and he would be terribly hurt, shocked, perhaps even disgusted, to realize what I was thinking.

Joshua was here, elderly, wise, concerned. I felt safe with him. That thought reminded me of William. William, now so drawn to Jessie, his square, hard face softened by her smile, his slow warm voice even warmer when responding to her.

It was pleasant in the Red Hen. The copper pots glowed in the sunlight that poured through the glassed-in porch. The bearded young man who served us seemed as worldly wise as ever.

When we had been served, Joshua said, "Now, Gabriella, take your time, and tell me what happened to you last night. Tell me everything that you remember."

As I hesitated, marshaling my thoughts, arranging indelible memories, he went on, "You are quite sure that you were not injured in any way?"

I nodded.

He gave a small relieved sigh. "If anything had happened to you . . . seriously I mean, then I should never have been able to forgive myself."

"It wouldn't have been your fault. You warned me."

"I must be the judge." His wrinkled face was so serious, his velvety eyes so stern that fear swept me. "Now, go on," he said.

I wanted to. Yet I remembered how the others had reacted when I cried out that I had been attacked. When, in that moment of fear, and shock, I had said what I believed to be true. I hesitated, fearful that he, too, would look at me with amused concern, and then offer me an explanation which I knew would never satisfy me. But Helen had obviously believed me. She had phoned him. He had believed her. He had come to me.

He said gently, "I have reason for asking. It isn't just idle curiosity, nor morbid interest. Surely you realize that, Gabriella."

I thought back to the unidentifiable sound that had awakened me. I told him about that. Then, quickly, in as few words as possible, with as little drama as I could manage, I told him the rest of it.

He sat very still, listening, his white encircled bald head tipped toward one side, his velvety eyes staring off into the distance.

At last, when I was silent, he heaved a deep sigh. But his face was full of acceptance, of belief.

"Yes," he whispered. "Yes. Yes. I was right to come to you then."

"I don't understand it," I told him. "I can't see why anyone there would hurt me, want to destroy me. But. . . ."

He raised his thin hand. "We must accept that as given. There was your fall from Nellie. Then there was Fernetta's death. It is all one. It all began a long time ago."

I felt faint hope then. Perhaps Joshua knew the answer. Perhaps he could tell me the name of my enemy.

"If only your mother had been able to do what she set out to do. To disappear forever from Cornell

House, from the Tyssons. Then this would never have happened."

"It's because I am back," I said. I felt as if every bone in my body had suddenly turned weak and watery. I stared at him. "Are you saying that Benjamin brought me back to . . . to kill me? Are you daring to imply that he. . . ."

"I don't know. We must consider all. . . ."

"No. No. I won't consider Benjamin. It can't be. He loves me. We're going to be married." I heard the thick anger in my voice. It struck me with surprise. Was that me, Gaby Tysson, usually so timid that to enter a room full of strangers was an ordeal? Could that be me? How had I managed to change so? When had I changed?

Joshua said, "Gabriella, what do you remember of your father's accident?"

"Nothing. Not much anyway."

"Try to go back in your mind," he suggested. "I realize that it happened a long time ago. I know that your impressions must be blurred. But is there anything, anything left of it at all?"

I began to tell him that I had forgotten it, wiped it out, that I could know nothing to tell him.

But suddenly there was a picture in my mind. I saw my father and mother, hand in hand, walking down the long terrace steps, then cutting across the meadows, laughing together. I trotted along with them, the sun warm on my face. Then I saw the three of us at Cornell Cottage, beside the corral fence.

Terrell and Johanna were there, and Bernard, too.

"That's all right, Terrell," my father had said. "You needn't. I don't expect you to play groom."

"I have to earn my keep," Terrell said silkily. "You've made it plain, that I, that Johanna, are not welcome here. You've made it plain enough that we're freeloaders. Well, I don't intend to be. I'll play groom, or whatever else you want, to keep a roof over Johanna's head and the head of the boy." Terrell walked stiff legged in his high boots, rigid shouldered, into the stable. Bernard followed him, limping. His face was still taped and bandaged. Soon they both came out leading Satan's Son. Terrell tossed the reins to my father, said, "Have a good ride, sir," and turned away.

My father mounted and trotted away. My mother and I started back to the house. On the high terrace, we paused, looked back. Terrell was on a horse, too. He rode toward the jagged cliffs.

Then Bernard was saying. "Rosalie, Denby's all wrong. And I don't know what to do. After all, Johanna is a Tysson. We mustn't forget that."

My mother replied in a shrill voice. "This is Denby's house and land. You brought them here with you."

"I had to, Rosalie. I couldn't help myself. And now I don't know what to do."

"You've never known, except to rely on Denby, and to gamble away whatever he gave you. That's how the trouble started. You have a beautiful wife in Sally, a wonderful child in Fernetta. Why can't you be satisfied with them?"

There was a space in time. Suddenly it was late afternoon. My mother stood on the terrace, staring across the meadows.

She whispered, "I'm afraid something's wrong. Denby never stays out this late."

Terrell set down a tall glass. He got to his feet. "Shall I have a look around, Rosalie? Shall I see if I can meet up with him?"

Sally's hands writhed in her lap. She said, "Denby would never have stayed out all day. We'd better get up a search party."

"Let Bernard and me go out first. We'll know what to do after that."

It was twilight. Lacy clouds were rimmed with darkening blue. Terrell and Bernard came riding across the meadow. They led a snorting highstepping Satan's Son, burdened with a lifeless thing.

My mother screamed and ran toward them.

There was confusion, anguish. Mother screamed, "It couldn't have happened! Not this way! Not this way!" in shrill, accusing tones. There was the funeral. Benjamin was there, slim and dark haired, standing behind his father and mother. Bernard's face was gray against the white of bandages and tapes he wore. Sandy haired, bulky shouldered William never said a word, as silent a witness as I myself was. Afterwards, they met in the library, the family, and Joshua Horn, and the two lawyers. My mother was white faced, still. That night she took me and ran away forever from Cornell House. . . .

The memory was sharp and clear now. It had all been there, hidden for these ten years within the intricate coils of my brain, stored for just this moment. It was up to me to use it, apply it, make of it what I could.

Joshua was saying, "Gabriella, Gabriella, what is it?"

I returned from the past, my heart thudding against my ribs. I said slowly, "Joshua, I don't know . . . I think . . . I think that my mother believed that my father was murdered. I think that's why she took me and ran away."

He let his breath out in a long whispery sigh. "What is it that you remember?"

I told him as quickly, briefly, as I could.

"You have no proof," he said regretfully when I had finished. "No proof at all."

I agreed. Then I said, "Still, there is the evidence of the attacks on me. Perhaps that is a kind of proof."

"Then you must do as I tell you. You must go away from here at once. I'll drive you to the city myself. I'll return to Cornell House and make your excuses for you. Or if not that, I'll simply say that you've gone away for a few days."

It was a suggestion I yearned with all my heart to accept. But I couldn't. I had to know the truth, and I had to either prove or forever lay at rest my suspicions of my family. Of . . . yes, at last, I admitted it to myself, of Benjamin.

Aloud, I said firmly, "I can't run away now. I must understand. I must find out what happened. Without that I'll never have an hour's peace as long as I live."

He looked at me for a long intent moment. Then he signalled the bearded waiter for the check. He absently paid it, then rose. We left untouched the coffee and cake we had ordered, and went out to the car.

"We'll go into the city now, Gabriella," he said.

At my sound of protest, he raised his hand.

"I can't run away," I insisted. Where was the timid Gaby Tysson I had once been, I wondered? And knew the answer. She had been outgrown in the moment that she knew she faced death. She was prepared now to fight, for life, for love.

He said, "You remembered the lawyers, the meeting in the morning room apparently. But you didn't understand what was happening then. Perhaps the legal language went over your head. Perhaps you didn't even listen, as upset as you were. You don't seem to know what's involved. I have felt, and William has felt, too, that perhaps it would be safer if you didn't know."

I said bleakly, "Perhaps he has his own reason for saying that."

Joshua put the car into motion. "Improbable, but possibly true," he agreed, but the reservation in his voice told me that he didn't believe that. As we drove slowly down the highway, he went on, "Gabriella, what the lawyers will tell you is this. When you turn twenty-one at the end of this week, you will automatically become heir to Cornell House."

I stared at him, shocked into speechlessness.

"Yes. It's true." He glanced at me. "Plainly your mother never told you."

"Never," I gasped. "I had no idea. . . ."

"She cared less for that fortune than for your life, it would appear.

"Bernard, by terms of your father's will, has been guardian, trustee, and executor of the estate, all these years."

I thought of Benjamin, the way we had met so soon before my birthday. Something sickened inside me. How could I suspect him? My love, my dark eyed, smiling love . . . I could not, I dared not examine the possibilities. And yet I couldn't ignore them.

"Joshua, does Benjamin know?"

The old man shrugged slightly, didn't answer.

That was when I remembered the card in my purse. I took it out, passed it to him. "We needn't go to the lawyers. You've told me just what they could have told me. But I do think we should go there."

He examined the card briefly, handed it back. "Craddock Detective Agency," he said, and the car seemed to leap forward as he pressed the accelerator more firmly.

It didn't take us long to get to the city. The agency was located only two blocks away from the Case Life and Casualty Building. When we passed it, I started at its concrete and glass and chrome, the stacked beehive. It was just a few weeks since I had last seen it, worked there, feeling like a bee among many other bees.

I closed my eyes, thinking of Jessie. I had met her when I applied for my job. She had paid no attention to me for months, then suddenly she had taken up with me. We had lunch together, and dinner. Then she gave me that premature birthday party at which I had met Benjamin. My eyes stung with tears, while I warned myself not to jump to ugly and unsupported conclusions.

Joshua grunted his satisfaction as he spotted a parking place and pulled into it. "Perhaps we can gain some insight here."

But Mr. Craddock of the agency had nothing to say. He was a big, hard eyed man, who listened suspiciously while I explained that I wanted to know if he had had a client who had been trying to trace me, trying to trace a Gabriella Tysson.

"Our work is confidential," he told me when I had finished. "Why do you want to know?"

Joshua broke in. "That's confidential, too."

"Sorry I can't help you," Mr. Craddock told him.

Joshua smiled slightly. He took out a checkbook. He said, "What's your standard fee, sir?"

Mr. Craddock frowned. Then, "Fifty dollars an hour."

Joshua wrote busily, then put the check on the big scarred desk. "Would it take you an hour to locate a family named Haley for me?"

Mr. Craddock's frown became a faint smile. "No. But I don't charge by the minute. It's a flat fifty an hour."

Joshua glanced at his pocket watch, then slipped it out of sight. "It's all yours, sir."

Mr. Craddock swiveled in his chair, reached for a file. Within a moment, he said, "Haley." He paused.

I held my breath, every muscle in my body suddenly rigid.

"Haley," he repeated. "Yes, here it is. Benjamin Haley. Cornell House, Berlin Hills, California. That suit you?"

Joshua nodded expressionlessly. His withered hand reached out, folded around my trembling fingers. I swallowed hard. Benjamin had come to Mr. Craddock for help in finding me. It had not been an accidental meeting through Jessie. It had been planned.

"I believe we still have some time left of the hour," Joshua said. "Tell me, sir, how do you go about locating a person?"

Mr. Craddock shrugged. "That depends. The best thing to do is contact the police."

"And if it were not a police matter?"

"Then you check the city directory, assuming that there's no telephone listing. After that the schools, employment agencies. . . ."

He went on, but I no longer listened.

Benjamin had come to him for help in locating me. I couldn't believe it. I cast frantically for some explanation. It occurred to me that Terrell, Bernard, even William could have used Benjamin's name, address. And then I remembered how I had met Benjamin. Benjamin. Not Terrell or Bernard or William.

When Joshua rose to go, I rose with him. I followed him blindly back to the car.

He asked, "Now do you see why you must not go back to Cornell House?"

I didn't answer him. Instead I suggested that we stop at the Case Life and Casualty Building. He agreed without questioning me.

Within a few minutes I was in the Personnel Office, the room in which I had first met Jessie. The other girls there welcomed me. When I asked about Jessie they said she had resigned rather suddenly, and gone away. No one knew where, but it was thought that she had a rich new boyfriend.

Shivering, with a suddening pounding headache, I returned to the lobby.

Joshua took one look at me and insisted that we stop in the coffee shop for something to drink and a few minutes rest while we decided what I must do.

I had already decided, but I didn't bother to tell him so. I was glad to have a little while in which to collect myself. We took a corner table, and a waitress came to hand us menus. I looked up, and with a start of shock, I realized that I was looking into Drago's glittering, black eyes.

>>

13

I REMEMBERED INSTANTLY the time that I had wanted to treat Jessie to lunch in the coffee shop, but she had insisted that it was too expensive, and demanded that we go to our usual cafeteria. Now I understood that she hadn't wanted me to see Drago.

I looked at her black, shining eyes, and imagined them made up with shadow, plastered with false lashes. I looked at her faintly smiling mouth and imagined it painted scarlet. I stared at her tall lithe body and imagined it swathed in a long red skirt, her shoulders draped in a shawl. Yes, Drago the gypsy fortune teller, was the waitress who stood before me, expectantly awaiting my order.

I made myself smile at her. I asked, "How long have you been a waitress?"

"Five years," she answered, staring at me. "Why?"

"Don't you remember me? I'm Gaby Tysson. A

few weeks ago you were at Jessie Davis' house. You told my fortune. A lovely one, too." I hadn't wanted to frighten her. I had made my voice light, teasing, admiring.

She grinned. "Oh, yeah. It was some joke, hunh? Jessie was always kidding me, you know. Me, with this mop of black hair, and these black eyes. And then she came in, said she'd pay me ten bucks for a few hours of pretending. She said you'd never know me. Not in a million years. I didn't think I'd get away with it. But I did, and it was a pretty good job, wasn't it?"

"You did a very good job," I whispered.

Jessie had known that old Gaby Tysson only a little while, but she had learned her well. She had seen the stars in her eyes, and known how to appeal to the romantic yearning they symbolized. She had arranged for the party, at which Gaby would meet Benjamin. She had arranged for Drago the fortune teller to set the stage. And Gaby had played the part assigned to her.

I shivered, huddled in the chair. Benjamin and Jessie. . . .

The black haired waitress brought us coffee.

Joshua insisted that I drink it.

While I forced it down, he repeated what he had said before. "You mustn't go back, Gabriella. Your mother took you away to avoid the danger she believed that you might be in. You mustn't invalidate her sacrifice."

But I was determined to return. I remembered my father's death, the long years through which my mother had suffered loneliness and illness. I remembered Fernetta's death.

Benjamin and Jessie. . . .

"I've got to know the truth," I told Joshua.

He gave in finally. Unwillingly, protesting all the way, he drove me back to Berlin Hills, to Cornell House.

When, in the parking area, he stopped to let me out, he said, "You must be very careful, Gabriella. You realize that someone here, I don't know who, and you don't know who, in spite of what seems to be Benjamin's part in this, suspects that you're a danger to him."

I blinked at Joshua. "What do you mean?"

"Gabriella, if it is true that, as it appears, Benjamin sought you out, and deliberately courted you for his own reasons, then the attacks on you, coming before the marriage, simply don't make sense. Unless of course there is another basis for them."

I let my breath out in a long sigh. Of course, of course, why hadn't I seen that myself? If Benjamin wanted to marry me because I was the heir to Cornell House, then I must survive. I must survive at least until I inherited what my father had left me.

"Then why, why would anyone want me. . . ." I couldn't say the words. I didn't have to. Joshua understood.

He said, "There are motives other than greed. I might, in this case, suggest fear. Fear of what you could remember about the past, Gabriella. What you have already remembered."

I closed my eyes briefly, wincing with sudden pain. "I'll be careful," I told him.

"You'll trust no one. No one, Gabriella."

I thought of Benjamin, his quick smile, his deep, dark, smiling eyes. I thought of Jessie, her warm laugh. I thought of Terrell and Johanna, and Sally and Bernard. "I won't trust anyone," I promised.

A few days passed quietly.

I felt armored by my knowledge, by the suspicion with which I achingly regarded Benjamin and Jessie. I wanted to confront them with what I knew, but I didn't dare to. I had to wait, to offer myself as a bait in a trap, hoping that I could evade the trap when sprung, and still learn the hand that triggered it. Perhaps I hoped to prove Benjamin and Jessie culpable of no more than an attempt to deceive me.

I waited, playing the part I had chosen for myself, playing it with a skill I had not known I could summon. Still, Benjamin said, "Darling, you've been so quiet these past few days, I worry about you. Have I. . . ."

"It's nothing," I told him quickly.

His dark brows drew down. He studied me quizzically. "But something is bothering you," he insisted. "Ever since your runaway adventure with Joshua Horn, I've known that you were troubled."

"Troubled? Why should I be troubled?" I sat up straighter, folded my hands in my lap. I forced myself to smile brightly. "It has nothing to do with Joshua. It's just that. . . ."

"That what, darling?"

"I don't know. Oh, I do, really. I feel so . . . so restless."

His mouth sperad in a warm smile. "Gaby, don't you think you've kept us both waiting long enough now? We could have been married if not for William's interference, and then your own silly dear stubbornness."

"Maybe," I agreed.

"Then shall we. . . ."

"Benjamin, I don't know." I twisted my hands together and the solitaire he had given me sparkled in the sunlight. It had been Johanna's, he had told me. And he had had it with him when he had me traced in the city. He had had it with him before he laid eyes on me. He'd said it was in the jewelers for repair, and he'd taken it out to put on my finger. It could be true. But it seemed more likely that he had been determined to become engaged to me before I even knew he existed, before he had even seen me himself. But I loved him, I told myself. I thought I did. So how could my mind be so filled with these terrible suspicions? If I loved him, why couldn't I trust him? What had happened to Drago's sweet promises? But Drago, I reminded myself, had been a phony, waiting tables, fortune telling as a joke for ten dollars. Her promises meant nothing. And what of Benjamin's promises? Did they mean nothing, too?

"I don't understand this, Gaby," he said. "I'm beginning to think that you're just playing with me for your own reasons."

I stopped him with a quick gesture. "Benjamin, please don't. Can't you see that I'm confused?"

"But why, darling? What's happened?"

I was silent. My throat was clogged with the need to weep—the need to blurt out my fears, my accusations, the knowledge which was my only armor.

He had deliberately traced me through the Craddock Detective Agency. He must have met Jessie in the Case personnel office, and between them they had arranged the meeting that took place. He had hurried me into the engagement, hurried me into leaving my job, into coming to Cornell House with him. He had never told me that I was my father's heir, that Bernard was simply the trustee and executor of the estate that would be mine when I turned twenty-one. It occurred to me then that he might not know that. But then a further question occurred to me. If he hadn't known it, why had he bothered to locate me?

The family had not welcomed me, nor wanted me. If anything it had tried to believe I was an impostor, and once I was accepted as the real Gaby Tysson a nail had been put under Nellie's saddle blanket and I had been thrown. Fernetta had warned me to leave, and she had been murdered. Had she died because she had tried to save me? And then there had been those horrible moments in the falling elevator, another attack on me.

I hadn't known then where the danger lay. I hadn't remembered the circumstances of my father's death. I hadn't remembered being a witness to what had happened—to the morning he went out to ride, followed by Terrell and Bernard. They had come back. But my father had not. Not alive.

Had the suspicion that I might have witnessed something that morning frightened someone? Was it, as Joshua had suggested, fear that I might finally remember, at Cornell House, what I *had* at last remembered? Or was it greed? Greed for the fortune I was to inherit? If I knew the answers to those questions, I would know from which direction I must expect the next attack.

But I didn't know. I couldn't imagine a means of protecting myself. I could only wait.

Benjamin sighed, got to his feet. "I know I oughtn't to be so impatient. But Gaby, it's difficult. I want us so badly to start our life together."

"Yes," I said. And it was true. It was what I wanted. But how could I marry him now? Now, with these terrible questions in my mind?

"Have your feelings for me changed?" he asked. "Is that it?" His voice dropped, "Gaby, do you want to go away? To leave me?"

I whispered, "Oh, Benjamin, no!"

It was true. Oh, it was so true. I wanted to love him still. I *did* love him still, I told myself.

Soon, soon I would know the truth. Somehow I would discover it. And he would be proven blameless. He had brought me here only because he loved me, wanted me for his wife.

Now he bent over me. He said softly, "Gaby, your real birthday's just a few days off. Did you think I'd forgotten it? How could I? When I've planned all along that we would celebrate it together, as man and wife."

I said miserably, "I don't know, Benjamin. I can't quite. . . ."

His voice was suddenly cold. He straightened. His dark brows drew together in a scowl. "You can't quite make up your mind to it? Is that it?"

I didn't answer him.

Jessie, suddenly with us, laughed, "Benjamin, you look like the wrath of God about to explode. What on earth are you bullying poor Gaby about?"

Benjamin's scowl faded. He said lightly, "I'm trying to badger her into a marriage she wants but doesn't want."

"No," I whispered. "No, Benjamin. That's not it."

It was hard to pretend, knowing what I knew. But I had to. I did. I allowed nothing to show on my face that would give Jessie and Benjamin the idea that I knew they were allied against me.

Jessie said briskly, "Benjamin, you do talk nonsense. You seem to think you've waited a long time.

Why, you've waited for Gaby for years, haven't you? Surely a few more days is nothing."

He gave her a grudging laugh. "Jessie, dear friend, you may be right. But I hardly think that you qualify to know the urgency that I feel."

"Oh, don't I?" she demanded. "Shows what you know." She linked her arm through mine, drew me to my feet. "Come on, sweetie, let's let this tempestuous lover cool off before he says something he's sorry for."

We left the terrace together, and went walking through the golden meadow.

Jessie said thoughtfully, "I begin to believe that maybe Benjamin's right, Gaby. I walked in just in time to keep him from blowing up. And I think I did manage to divert him. But I have to tell you the truth, sweetie, you're making a terrible mistake. I'm afraid you have no intention of marrying him. I'm terribly afraid that you're going to hurt him."

It was too much to bear. Without thinking, pushed beyond caution, I burst out, "Jessie, Jessie, you must stop playing with me." With those words said, it was too late to hold back.

Jessie stopped, the meadow grass waving around her, cast shadows on her face, depths into her green eyes. "What are you talking about?"

"You must know," I told her.

"Know what?"

"Please don't lie any more. I know that Benjamin used detectives to locate me. A man named Craddock sent him to the Case offices, and that must be how he met you. That's when you two became friendly, and when you took up with me, and then arranged the party with Drago, the waitress from the first floor coffee shop, to play the fortune teller. It was none of it an accident. I know that, Jessie."

I don't know exactly what I expected her to do. I only know that I was shaken with surprise and doubt at her reaction.

She grinned, "Gaby, you're such an innocent. Benjamin remembered you from when you were a kid. He was always curious about you, always wondered what had happened to you. So he located you. But he didn't know where it would lead. So he enlisted my services. He wanted to be able to back out, drop it, if you weren't the Gaby Tysson he'd cared about all his life."

"Cared about?" I repeated.

"Of course. That was what was behind it. That's why he never married. He always had the feeling that you ... and he ..."

"But we scarcely knew each other," I protested. "How could he. . . ."

"He's older than you by seven years. His memory is better than yours, I suspect. Though I don't think it would be politic on your part to tell him that you don't remember him from your childhood. It might hurt his feelings, you know."

"But I do remember him. Just a little. I know it was Benjamin, but somehow. . . ." I stopped. I had only known Benjamin for two weeks. That was how long the Haleys had been in Cornell House before my father died, and my mother took me away.

I concealed what I was thinking. That it had been a good try on Jessie's part, a quick clever answer to my accusations. But I couldn't accept her explanation.

She said, "So now you know all about it. As for Drago . . . well, that was just a fun touch. I've used her as fortune tell before. She looks the part so. I knew you'd enjoy it."

It seemed plausible, Benjamin's search for me based on a memory, Jessie's involvement. She loved excitement, mystery, romance. She loved to direct other people's lives. Oh, yes, it made sense. A kind of sense. Except that I knew there was more to it than that. No one, not Benjamin, not Sally or Bernard, or Johanna or Terrill, had told me that within a few days I would own Cornell House. Still, I knew I must try to recoup by pretense what I had lost by folly.

I said, "Jessie, forgive me. I had the funniest feeling that you and Benjamin were up to something, and I. . . ."

Jessie gave a hoot of disbelieving laughter. "Me and Benjamin! Oh, sure. Of course. Me and Benjamin. Especially now that I've met William. I tell you, Gaby. I don't think you have eyes in your head."

And that was true, too, I knew. I knew that Jessie had been pursuing William at full steam and he didn't appear to be attempting to retreat from her with much determination.

The thought was unpleasant, but I told myself that I had no right to resent William's interest in Jessie, nor Jessie's interest in him.

We had reached the pines by then. The scent was strong and sweet, the shade pleasant.

Jessie chuckled, "I guess we were silly to do it the way we did. But we didn't mean any harm."

I didn't answer. But I found myself wondering what would have happened if I had married Benjamin before we returned together to Cornell House.

What would have happened to me after my birthday?

It was a speculation I couldn't bear. I had no reason to turn against Benjamin. I had every reason to believe he loved me. I wanted to prove that the unknown enemy was not Benjamin, but one of the others.

I stopped, plucked a handful of pine needles from the ground, and turned back, suddenly in a hurry. I wanted to be with him, to talk to him. I wanted to reassure myself. Joshua had warned me to trust no one. No one at all. But I had to trust Benjamin.

Jessie cried, "Hey, what's with you? We've been dawdling along for almost an hour, and now, suddenly, you've practically started running."

"I wanted to go back, to talk to Benjamin."

Jessie gave an exaggerated pant. "Well, okay, but do you mind if I take it easy? I'm on vacation, you know, not in training for an Olympics race."

I didn't mention it, but I suddenly recalled that I'd been told in the office that Jessie had quit her job, gone away, that she had a rich boyfriend. She wasn't on vacation. And the rich boyfriend was. . . .

I turned away, walking quickly. I didn't want to have to answer her.

Then I was suddenly swept by dizziness. My vision blurred. The pines seemed to spin around me, and gave out a shrill, rustling sound. A quivering rippled through me and I fell. At the same time, Jessie yelped, "Good grief, what's going on? Oh, darn it! Now I've hurt my ankle."

I pushed myself to my feet, hurried back to her. "Let me see."

But she clasped her ankle in both hands and rocked back and forth. "Darn it, Gaby. It hurts like fire. And I can't figure out what happened. One minute I was okay, and the next I thought the ground was dancing around under me."

I knew that I had had the same sensation. I couldn't see the jagged cliff wall above the ocean through the pines, nor the raw, broken apart place where Lovers Leap had been. But I thought of it, and guessed what had happened.

The area had been shaken by a small earth tremor. A follow up, perhaps, of the ones it has had back in February.

I didn't say anything to Jessie. She was already too upset. Her green eyes sparkled with tears, and her face was pale. She begged, "Gaby, see if you can find William, or Benjamin. I don't think I can stand without any help."

I raced through the pines, intending to short cut across the meadow to the cottage. I was almost there when I heard a loud yell, then another. And suddenly, Devil's Dancer, and the giant palomino, and Nellie came pounding toward me, heavy hooves thudding, manes flying.

Momentarily I stopped, not knowing which way to go, how to escape them. Then I swerved away, and stumbled, with the horses almost upon me. Even as I fell, I felt arms come around me, rolling me away through veils of dust, away from the hammer of the thundering hooves.

William held me close, his body half over me.

The horses went by, went streaming across the meadow and into the pines.

Still William's arms held me. I felt safe, happy. I felt bewildered, too. And then, realizing what a close shave I had had, I forgot everything else. I drew myself away, straightened up.

"Where did they come from?" I asked.

"I don't know," William said, his silver eyes thoughtful.

"But you were. . . ." I stopped myself. I got to my feet, painfully brushed the dust from my trousers.

William rose, too, looked down at me, his mouth compressed. "I was what?"

"You were at the corral, weren't you?"

"Why do you ask?"

I didn't answer him.

He said, "You interest me," He paused. Then, "We've just had a good earth shiver, and you ask me where I was. I wondered why." When I didn't say anything, he went on, "Did you think I spooked the horses in the corral, and set them out to stampede over you? Is that it?"

Still I didn't answer.

"Now you know that you're in danger, don't you? You know that you must let me take you away from here."

"I can't leave." I wished I could tell him why. I wished I dared trust him. But I had promised Joshua that I would trust no one. And if I didn't trust Benjamin, then how could I trust William?

He said suddenly, "All right, Gaby. I'll tell you. I was following you. I've been just a few feet away from you and Jessie the whole time. When she hurt her ankle, I almost showed myself, but you started back, so I went after you."

I had completely forgotten about her in the fright of the racing horses. But he had reminded me. "Oh, William, you'd better go back to her. Why didn't you. . . ."

That was when she came limping out of the pines,

started toward him, calling, "What's all that noise? What happened?"

William said under his breath, "Be careful, Gaby. Watch out for the next couple of days, will you?" Then, with a wide, slow smile, he went to meet Jessie, saying, "Never mind the noise, girl. It's all over now. But what happened to *you*?"

14

THEN TERRELL, RIDING a bay and looping his rope as he came, trotted up to us. He jerked his horse to a stop, leaned from the saddle. "Did you see them?"

I nodded. "They were heading toward the pines."

"Did you feel the tremor? They sure did. They spooked and took off. Some fool left the corral gate open, I suppose." He spurred the horse, nodded at me, and galloped away.

I went on toward Cornell Cottage, Jessie and William were a few steps behind me. She was hanging on his arm and limping, but laughing too.

I tried to remember the exact sequence of events. Jessie had fallen back, protesting that I was walking too fast. I had felt the ground shake under me and fallen. She had cried out that she'd hurt her ankle, and then the horses had come thundering across the meadow toward me. William pulled me to safety.

If he hadn't been following us, hidden—and why
had he done that—I would be dead by now. I would
be a threat to no one.

Bernard was near the corral. His face was red,
the scar brilliant. He ground his hands together as
if they ached. There was a quaver in his voice
when he said, "There you are. I wondered where
you where when it happened. Did you feel it?"

"It was scary," I said. "And Jessie's hurt her
ankle."

"The horses. . . ."

"How did they get out?"

"I don't know. I suppose the gate wasn't properly
shut. They panicked, as they do sometimes."

I had the feeling that it hurt him to talk, that the
words were being forced out through some obstruc-
tion in his throat.

"They almost ran me down," I told him. "If William hadn't happened to be there. . . ."

I stopped then. I heard the sound of the drumming hooves. I felt William's arms suddenly around
me.

Bernard said, "Gabriella, you're my niece. You're
Denby's only daughter. You played with Fernetta
when the two of you were children. I . . . I don't
know what to tell you. I just can't go on this way.
But I don't know. . . ."

Johanna came out of the cottage at that moment.
She walked briskly across the small distance. She
leaned against the corral fence, and put her hand on
Bernard's arm. "Bernard," she said softly, "Bernard,
are you all right? You look . . . I must say that you
don't look well to me. Your color . . . it reminds me
. . . I think you should go up to the house and lie
down."

Her interruption was firm and complete. Plainly whatever he had been going to tell me would not be told now. He said shakily, "I'm all right, Johanna." Now his face was ashen, his eyes swollen.

She went on, "You look like that time in Las Vegas, when Terrell and I. . . ."

"Yes, yes. But I'm all right."

Despite what he said he looked like a man on the verge of collapse, a man so fear ridden that he had become a puppet, dancing while another pulled the strings. It was a moment of insight that I carefully stored away for future reference, another piece to the puzzle.

She said sweetly, "You push yourself too hard. You worry much too much. You ought to take it easier, Bernard. Why, ever since Fernetta's suicide. . . ."

He winced at her unnecessary cruelty, said, "Never mind, Johanna."

I considered what she had said. It seemed to me that Bernard already took it as easy as any man could. He had nothing to do. If he made a decision, I didn't know about it. Cornell House, and those who lived there, seemed supported and directed more by Terrell Haley than by Bernard. But Bernard was trustee and executor under my father's will.

Johanna had turned her attention to me. "You haven't been here, have you?"

I shook my head.

"Then where were you?"

"Jessie and I took a walk in the meadow. You saw us leave."

"Oh, yes, that is right, isn't it? You didn't open the corral gate, did you?"

"I wasn't near it." I stared at Johanna, taken aback by the implication.

Johanna said smoothly, "No, of course. I suppose not. Still . . . it does seem that someone here is prone to malicious mischief. And we never had any trouble before you came."

I touched the solitaire Benjamin had given me. I wished he were somewhere about now. Not somewhere about, but here, to defend me. I didn't know what to say.

Bernard muttered, "Johanna, don't be ridiculous."

She shrugged, "Terrell is so upset. You know how he feels about the horses, about the whole place, Bernard. And how he feels about Benjamin. The boy is kept dangling, while Gaby suits her own purposes, whatever they are. I can't help but wonder what is really in her mind." She gave me a bright straight look. "You do understand me, don't you?" When I didn't answer, she said gently, "I'm a mother. I worry about my son. I see how he feels, how hurt he is. Why don't you set a date for your wedding, Gaby? What's holding you back?"

I could have answered her simply. I could have said that fear was holding me back. I wasn't sure of Benjamin. I suspected him of something too terrible to contemplate. I kept hoping that he was a victim as much as I, but the doubt was there, not to be denied, nor ignored.

The cottage door slammed. Benjamin came out. "I've been listening to the radio. There have been tremors all up and down the coast, not just here."

He came down to me, slipped an arm around my shoulder. "Don't look so upset. Nothing will happen. It didn't leave more than a trace on the Richter scale."

Johanna said, "Oh, I don't think Gaby's worried about that. She was in the meadow when the horses stampeded."

I thought of Jessie and William, still in the meadow, alone together. What were they talking about? Planning?

It seemed to me that with William's coming my life at Cornell House had been turned upside down. Had he tried to have me killed in the fall from Nellie? Had he lured me into the elevator? Had he left the corral gate open when he followed Jessie and me into the meadow? No one mentioned it now. No one seemed to think of it. But I knew that if the gate had been properly closed, the tremor might have sent the horses stampeding inside, but they would never have broken free to go thundering away in panic.

If it had been William, if his saving me not once but twice, his concern for me, was all pretence, then what was his motive? To think of him as the shadowy figure at the center of evil around me hurt oddly. Much the same as when I tried to imagine Benjamin in that role. But I knew that Benjamin had deceived me. I knew that he had traced me through the Craddock Detective Agency, met me through Jessie in a deliberately planned scheme. I knew that Jessie, too, had deceived me. She had lied about being on vacation. She had quit her job, come to Cornell House. For a moment, I couldn't see why. But then it was plain. I had delayed my marriage to Benjamin. It was her job to persuade me to go through with it. Her job to be confidante and friend to me, and to keep me from changing my mind. How ugly it all seemed. I wished I could go back to being that wide eyed Gaby I had been before I came to Cornell

House, that timid girl living with her dreams. But there was no going back. There hadn't been since the day that I felt the mists of death rise up around me.

Benjamin drew me close, whispered, "Gaby, what is it?"

I managed to smile. I had learned how to dissemble. I said, "Nothing's the matter. I'm going up to the house to change. Okay?"

He let me go. "I'll check the radio again, and see what's happening now."

I left him, with Bernard and Johanna, at the cottage, and slowly climbed the multiple terraces to the house. There, at the front door, I turned. I looked across the valley.

It was bathed in sunshine. The long, sloping meadows fringed with the jagged teeth of the lichen frosted rocks blended against the horizon, seeming as permanent as the rim of blue ocean beyond and as secure as the covering sky. Peace lay like a beautiful blanket over the sweet retreat.

Yet here my father died, strangely, uselessly, in what I no longer believed to have been an accident. And it was from here that my mother had fled. Here blue eyed Fernetta had fallen to her death from the raw place once called Lovers Leap. And here I myself had repeatedly faced terror since my return. Disillusion and terror.

A part of me yearned to run away, to turn my back on Benjamin, on Cornell House, forever. A part of me urged me to leave William and Jessie behind. A part of me whispered that I must forget Bernard and Sally, Johanna and Terrell. Something in me pleaded for safety.

But there was something else in me, too, I realized.

There was a steel I hadn't known I had. It had been my mother's steel, what she used to build a new life for the two of us once she had left Cornell House behind. It was the steel I remembered in my father.

I refused to give up. I knew that I must learn what happened here, I must claim my heritage, or else I must allow myself to sink back into the dream of life that I had once accepted as real.

I turned briskly, went into the house.

Helen, gray-white hair more wispy than usual, popped out of the morning room. I knew she had been waiting there, hoping to catch me alone.

She gave the hall a quick look up and down, said expectantly, "Joshua Horn called you, Gaby."

"I'll call him back," I said.

"Listen, love. I'd better tell you. He misunderstood me at first. I told him you were out with Jessie. And he took that to mean that you and Jessie had left. He was . . . well, love, the word is overjoyed. He immediately asked me if you'd given me an address. We had a funny few minutes then. With me not knowing what he was talking about and him not knowing what I was talking about. Finally we got ourselves sorted out. And then he was so disappointed, love." She paused. Then, whispering, she went on, "He's terribly frightened for you, love."

I thought of the album on my bed, the detective agency card. It was that which had led me to my suspicions of Benjamin, of Jessie. I took a wild stab at a possible truth. I asked, "Helen, you left the Craddock card for me to find, didn't you?"

Her lined face seemed to shrink. She didn't answer me.

"Joshua Horn and I went there," I told her.

"Then you know," Helen quavered.

"I only know Benjamin set out to trace me and did," I said firmly.

Helen whispered, "It was time. It had to be."

"But why? Why, if I'd been gone so long. . . ."

"Your birthday, love. The estate." Helen gave the hallway a fearful look. "Listen, love, two, maybe three years ago, Bernard was going to do it. Then Fernetta had that terrible fall steeplechasing, and was crippled. Bernard and Sally, occupied with the girl, they forgot about it, you see. But now. . . ."

"The estate?" I repeated.

"This is a bad place," she said. "I've known it all these years. Always, always. It's been a bad place ever since your father died. Your mother knew it at once. I helped her. I helped her go away. Knowing that's why she must. All these years, love, I wondered, hoped, prayed life was good to you, never expecting to see you again, and knowing, as your mother did, that it would be safer for you that way."

"If you know that, then you must know why. You must know what my mother feared."

"No." But Helen's face had gone from pale to gray. Her lips were blue. Her eyes seemed to recede into her round wrinkled face. "Maybe it's an old wickedness come to roost. Maybe it's sin growing like weeds where there is no love. But for you, can't you see it? don't you feel it? It's a dangerous and deathly place to be."

I knew. It was Cornell House, the estate, the fortune it entailed. If I were alive to inherit it, it would be all mine. Benjamin had brought me here to marry me. Or had he brought me here to ensure my death?

I realized something that had never occurred to me before. If I hadn't been found, then Bernard would have had to go to the courts, to request that

I be declared dead, so that the estate would become his. Was that why Benjamin had sought me out? Had he and Bernard decided between them that I must marry Benjamin, or else die?

I was sickened at the thought, but I knew that I mustn't close my eyes to any possible truth. Suddenly I saw a way in which I could force the issue, a way in which I could learn, once and for all, what I had to know.

"Leave now, love," Helen whispered. "I've said too much as it is. Leave now because that's what your mother wanted for you."

It would have been so easy then to say, "Oh, yes, Helen, you're right. I'm terrified and I can't bear it. Oh, yes, call Joshua and have him come and get me. Let's go up now and pack my things." It would have been easier than anything in the world.

Instead, I said, "I can't, Helen. Try not to worry."

I turned to the stairs, my eyes avoiding the boarded up elevator in which I had nearly died, the elevator which had taken Fernetta to her awful death.

Sally, a wraith of the woman she had been on the day I arrived, looked out of the room at the end of the corridor. "Where's Bernard?"

"At the corral with the others."

"Is he all right, Gabriella?"

"I think so."

"I worry about him," Sally whispered. "He was a good man. You must believe me that he was always a good man." Her voice shook. "And now . . . now . . . it isn't his fault. It's yours. Yours. If you hadn't returned. . . ." She raised wide, horrified eyes to stare at me, as if she realized what she was saying.

Then she stepped back. She slammed the door. I heard the key turn in the lock.

Sally had closed herself away again, closed herself in with her whiskey and her fear.

I went on towards my own room. The pale, blue one I had lived in as a child. Yes, yes, it was just as Sally said. It had all begun with my return to Cornell House. . . .

But it would be over soon. I knew what I must do. That day, and the next, passed quietly. I waited, tense and suspicious, for something to happen, waited for the opportunity I needed to present itself. Even the house, the terraces and meadows, were sunk in stillness.

The only sound was Jessie's joyful laughter as she teased William, it seemed to me. The only warmth was in the smile Benjamin bent on me.

I had spoken to Joshua, reassured him as well as I could. Even as I did, careful of what I said, I thought I heard faint breathing on the line. Once again someone was listening in on my conversation with him. Once again someone was concerned when I was in contact with him. Several times he had come to the house, only to be turned away, without my being told, until too late, that he had been there. When William had offered to take me to him, the car had been tampered with. Joshua Horn was too knowledgeable about Cornell House, it seemed, for me to be allowed to see or speak to him. Yet, each time, when I had insisted, I had managed to do that.

I knew what I must do. But when I tried to think, to understand, it seemed that my mind was a blank void. I wanted the truth, I needed it, but I was afraid of it, too. I was terribly afraid of what I would learn.

So I waited, knowing I was the bait, for the right opportunity to come along.

Then, quite suddenly, my twenty-first birthday loomed ahead of me. It would be the next day. I had looked forward to it for years for no extraordinary reasons—until now. I had already celebrated it once, with Jessie laughing at me, and Benjamin, that tall, dark, handsome Benjamin, smiling at me from across the room, and Drago hoarsely announcing love and fortune and a beautiful future, all for ten dollars and a practical joke.

How it hurt when I allowed myself to think of that now.

My chance came at last. It was late, dark. Benjamin suggested that we take a walk together. The house had seemed to sway once when we were at dinner. He dismissed the movement as one more of those small shocks that had touched the area in the last few days. But he thought it would be pleasant to take a look around.

I remembered what Joshua Horn had told me. *Trust no one. No one at all.*

I remembered the near misses I had had before.

But this was my chance. I decided to take it.

I was terribly afraid, but I knew that I mustn't turn back.

15

I WENT WITH him.

We moved idly along the terraces, stepping from level to level, then past Cornell Cottage, and into the quiet meadow.

Benjamin's lean face was touched with moonlight. His dark eyes gleamed at me, and his smile flashed. He said, "It's a beautiful night, isn't it? And it's good this way, Gaby, to be alone. It seems to me that lately, always, we've never had a chance to be together. Just the two of us. Together as we should be."

"It's quiet. Almost too quiet. As if we're in the lull before the storm," I said.

He tilted his dark head to look up at the sky. "There's no storm in sight," he answered.

I wondered. I felt the pressure of stillness almost as a weight on me. I felt the pressure of fear bearing down, nearly crushing me. With all my heart, I wanted to turn back now. To run for the house, the lights, the safety I might find there.

But I made myself walk on beside him.

The jagged teeth of the cliffs reared against the sky—between them, the vast empty place where the rock called Lovers Leap had fallen away, the place where Fernetta had died.

It was there, to that very place, that Benjamin led me, and I allowed him to do so.

Even then, I told myself that I loved him and trusted him. It was for that reason that I must test him. To learn the explanation for his deceit. To learn from him who the shadowy figure was that manipulated us all at Cornell House.

We stood at the point where the slide had begun months before, and together we looked down at the shore below, at the raw and shattered rock, at the curling lips of the ocean waves that flung up vast veils of white spume as they rolled in.

When the moon sheltered behind clouds, the scene below us disappeared. When the moon returned, the scene below seemed sharper, more clear, closer, than it had been before.

I shivered involuntarily.

He said, "Don't worry, Gaby. There won't be another slide here. Lightning never strikes twice in the same place."

I made myself laugh. I said lightly, "At least that's what we'd like to believe, isn't it, Benjamin?"

"Perhaps," he agreed.

Then, twisting the solitaire on my finger, I said, "Benjamin, remember that I told you I thought we ought to make plans for after our marriage?"

"Yes, darling, I do remember."

"Have you thought about it?"

"Oh, some. Not very hard."

I thought I heard a sound somewhere nearby. A whisper of movement. Nothing more than that. I didn't mention it to Benjamin. I didn't dare to.

"You should have. Because I will never live here."

"Oh? Why not?"

"I couldn't bear it. Too much has happened. We must go away together, just you and I, alone. I never want to see Cornell House again."

"How curious," he said dryly. "Just like your mother."

I didn't answer him.

"Poor relations," he said. "That's what the Haleys have always been. Money will make men do strange things, darling."

Once again, from the darkness, I heard a sound, the faint clink of a rolling stone. I felt the threat envelop me. I felt danger creep quietly closer. I held myself still and felt Benjamin's arms tighten around me. I held my hand and the solitaire sparkled in the moonlight. I drew it off, handed it to him.

"I can't marry you, Benjamin. I'm sorry. It would never work."

He held me close still. He was silent for a heart-beat, two heartbeats.

I raised my eyes to his, waiting.

He said, "You've turned against me."

I made a small sound of protest, and terror held me frozen within his arms.

"Turned against me, Gaby. And spoiled it all. The plans, Gaby. The hope. The dreams. We could have had it all. And now you've spoiled it. What could have been so perfect is gone."

His arms slid from my shoulders. His fingers crept up, touched my throat lightly.

I felt the tension in his body, heard it in his voice.

I found myself unwillingly moving away from him—away from him, and closer to the broken rim of Lovers Leap.

"Why did you do it?" I pleaded, knowing my danger, and seeking a delay.

"You know the answer to that, Gaby. Perhaps you always knew and pretended not to. The estate, of course. Tomorrow it would have been yours. And mine. Now it will never be yours. You do realize what you've done? I tried to save you, you see. When Craddock found you for me, and I had a good look at you, one day you never even knew about, outside the Case Building, I made a quick change in plans. Before it had seemed so simple. All we needed was proof that we had searched for you, and not found you. Then we could have gone to court, had you declared dead, and Bernard would have been the natural heir. But when I did find you, it was a shock. Until that day I saw you. Then it became even simpler. We would marry. You would inherit. I could have loved you. We could have been happy together."

I whispered, "Benjamin, how could Bernard lend himself to this . . . this. . . ."

"Oh, Bernard is a weakling, and Sally's a drunk. He's no match."

"Then it was you who. . . ."

"Poor Gaby. No, no. I never tried to hurt you. I wanted to marry you. That was to be my way."

I tried to ask then, who, if not him, if not Bernard . . . but the fingers were tightening around my throat.

Benjamin said, "I'm sorry. I'm sorry that this has all been too much for you. It's a weakness in your family, of course. Both on your father's side and on your mother's. Everyone knows about it. They always have. Even poor Bernard . . . so you see, it will make sense when they find you. You've been on edge lately, pale, somewhat morose. You couldn't face marriage, nor life with a man, with me. Your recognition of your plight, and your empty future, led you here. Oh, Gaby, it could have been different. I'm shattered. My life will never be the same without you."

I clung to him, fastening my hands around his belt. I whispered, "You'll have Jessie to console you, won't you, Benjamin?"

"Oh, Jessie . . . yes, perhaps."

I could feel his muscles tighten, then felt myself launched wildly forward, while I still gripped at him, at his belt, the only support I had. His fingers had closed around my throat. I could hardly breathe now. Then, suddenly, off balance and tumbling, with the picture in my mind of the rock strewn beach below me, I found myself torn in two. I was being thrust over the edge of Lovers Leap, and I was being bodily hauled away from it. I fought for the freedom I needed, fought to breathe, fought for solid earth under my feet.

I spun away, with dirt sliding beneath my heels, my hands torn from Benjamin's belt. He tumbled past me. I felt his body brush mine, the movement of air it created. I dropped to the ground in the same moment. I heard Benjamin's great long despairing scream.

Then there was silence. A terrible empty silence.

I lay, my legs dangling in space, my fingers frozen into the arm that encircled me. I lay, breathing hard, with my heart pounding.

William said, "Dear God, I almost lost you."

"Benjamin," I whispered. "I gave him back the ring. I told him I wouldn't marry him."

"I heard it. I almost waited too long."

"Someone was there. I knew it, sensed it. I didn't realize it was you. I thought it might be. . . ."

William's arms moved carefully, never letting me go for a second. He slid back. He angled his body along the edge. He drew me with him.

At last solid earth was under me. But I couldn't stop shaking. Not even when he raised me to my feet, steadied me, held me. I just kept shaking.

"More tremors," he said. "Don't let them worry you. It's over, Gaby. You're all right. I know that Benjamin's death is. . . ."

"I feel as if it's the end of the world," I answered.

"Not of the world," he told me. "The end of something evil. Something evil that's gone on for much too long."

He led me through the dark.

We passed Cornell Cottage without speaking. I didn't dare look at the black windows. I didn't dare think of what Terrell and Johanna might be doing, planning.

Beyond that place, William said, "We'll call the police first. Do you understand?"

I nodded.

At the lower terrace a shadow moved and took form. It came limping to meet me, meet William.

"Benjamin, Benjamin. . . ." It was Jessie's voice, but raw with fright. "Where is Benjamin?" she demanded.

The moonlight suddenly spilled onto her face. Her eyes gleamed wildly. Her hair was disarrayed. Her long, slim body shook with a thick, rapid trembling that reminded me terribly of a trapped and dying bird I had once held when I was a child.

"Benjamin. . . ." Jessie said one last time.

William stared at her for a moment. Then he said very quietly, "He tried to throw Gaby off Lovers Leap when she broke her engagement to him. I was watching. In the struggle, I'm afraid he fell himself."

She seemed frozen except that her body trembled, and her lips worked convulsively. Her gleaming eyes raked him up and down, then turned to me. "You ruined it all. It was a perfect plan."

"Except that it didn't work," William told her.

"All of it, the house, the land, the money, it would all have been Benjamin's. Terrell's and Benjamin's. He came into the office, and he sat across from me, asking about you. How bright his eyes were, how wonderful his smile. It seemed so easy then. I helped him meet you. I wanted to. It happened so quickly. One minute he was a stranger, from out of nowhere, a wonderful and exciting stranger. And then we were lovers, Gaby. Yes, lovers. Benjamin and I. You didn't have all of him. No matter what you thought. You never even had the most of him. It was the money. He knew what he was doing."

I winced, but there was more I had to know. There was someone else . . . someone who had killed, killed again. . . . I put my pain aside. I said, "But when Benjamin brought me back here. . . ."

"I don't know anything. Not anything." She shrank back. "You can't say I did. Just about Benjamin wanting to marry you. And after you came here with him, he called me. He said you were stalling and that I ought to come down. I was glad to. I wanted to be with him." Her eyes flashed at William.

"I suppose you thought I cared about you. But that was a blind. It was really Benjamin."

He didn't answer her.

"It would have all been all right," she said. "He wouldn't have hurt you. If only you'd married him."

Like a sleepwalker, she turned, went down along the terrace path.

We saw her moving. We saw her get into her car. We didn't try to stop her.

We went up to the house.

I sat beside the window in the morning room, looking down at the dark cottage.

William went to call the police, then came and stood beside me. "I've told Bernard and Sally."

The two of them soon joined us. They held hands like bewildered and frightened children, but they were old, withered, destroyed.

They sank into the sofa. Bernard said, "You'd better know it all, Gabriella."

I swallowed hard, bent my gaze away from him. I didn't want to know any more.

But he went on, "It started so long ago. In Las Vegas, it was. I liked the gambling too much. I got into trouble. Johanna and Terrell happened to be there and they managed to extricate me from what was a pretty messy situation. I brought them back here at their insistence. After all, Johanna was a Tysson. It seemed all right. I couldn't know. But your father was angry. Angry at the mess I'd made with the gambling, and angry with me for having brought the Haleys here. He didn't trust Terrell. He felt that Terrell might have deliberately involved me in Las Vegas, just to play hero. We had an argument. The Haleys said they'd go. But they stalled. Then your father was killed. He was murdered,

Gabriella. I'm sure of it. I'm sure Terrell did it. But he said I did it. We had been riding together that day, you know. He said we alibied each other. If I'd accuse him, then he would accuse me. It was a stalemate. I did nothing.

"Your mother suspected the truth. When she learned the terms of the will, she feared for your life. Wisely. She took you and ran away. I made no effort to find her, or you. Not for years. Then I couldn't stand it any more. I decided to trace you. Secretly. Carefully. So Terrell wouldn't know." He paused, breathed a long deep rasping breath.

In the pause, Sally said, "Bernard's a good man. He always was. But. . . ."

"They found out. They watched me always, so they knew what I was going to do. Fernetta went steeplechase riding with Terrell, without my permission, and she fell. I knew what it meant. My child was crippled for life as a warning to me. I gave up the idea of looking for you. Then, as your twenty-first birthday approached, Terrell and Johanna decided something would have to be done. They'd have to be able to prove you couldn't be traced. Benjamin set out to do that and found you instead. He changed the plans, and brought you back. Terrell was in a rage. He knew you'd been present when your father told him he'd have to leave. He was afraid of what you might remember. I didn't have the courage to try to stop him, not even when I realized he must have done something to Nellie to make her throw you. But Fernetta did have the courage." He stopped again.

Sally sobbed into her hands.

"Fernetta called me to come, to protect you," William said.

"Helen told me that," I answered.

Bernard said, "So Terrell killed her. I didn't care about anything after that. How he did it, I don't know. But I'm sure he did."

"A good man," Sally whispered behind her twisted hands. "Blackmailed all these years. Terrified all these years."

"A craven coward," Bernard said hoarsely. "But it's over now. Thank God it's over now. And you're safe, Gabriella. You're safe at least."

I saw lights line the crest of the mountainside and spill over, sweeping around to the curves of the dirt road that led into the valley. I got to my feet.

The floor seemed to shake under my feet.

I felt a tremor in my pulses, in my body, I felt myself falling.

William caught me. We clung together.

The chandelier in the hallway tinkled wildly. The lights suddenly went out.

The house shivered and shook.

Somewhere a pane of glass burst with a terrible noise. I was on the floor then, with William shielding my body. I heard Sally cry out. I heard Bernard moan.

Then a great deafening roar went up, echoing along the hillside, along the sloping meadows.

There was a heaving and rending. Debris pelted the house.

As suddenly as it had begun it was over.

Silence fell, a deep humming breathless silence.

I got to my feet with William's help.

Bernard lay crumpled on the sofa, his mouth hanging open, his eyes wide. Sally huddled beside him, stroking his hand. There was no color in his lips, his face. Even his scar was white. I knew that he was dead.

Swaying dizzily, I turned to the window, to peer into moonlit darkness.

The jagged line of the cliffs had changed. It was impossible to see the place where Lovers Leap had once been. The surrounding rocks had fallen away. The dark of the sky shone through.

Below that sky was an unbelievable emptiness. Cornell Cottage was gone. The cottage, corral and stables, had slid down into the ocean. Johanna and Terrell were with Benjamin now.

Headlights swept the house, turning into the parking area. A red dome ray blinked off and on.

"The police," William said.

He took my hand. We went down to meet them together.

I knew that I had awakened from a dream when I felt the mists of death around me, and unknowingly walked into a nightmare. Now I was awakened from nightmare, and Drago's prophecy had come true after all. I would have love and a future with William. It was all I wanted.

*A LOVE THAT SPANNED
TWO CONTINENTS...*

*AND A PASSION
THAT WOULD NOT BE STILLED*

CHINA
SHADOW

CLARISSA ROSS

A stormy epic of adventure and desire set in England and the exotic
Orient . . . a tempestuous romantic
novel in the tradition of MOOR-
HAVEN!

21055/$1.75

Where better paperbacks are sold, or directly from
the publisher. Include 25c per copy for mailing;
allow three weeks for delivery. Avon Books, Mail
Order Dept. 250 West 55th Street, New York,
N.Y. 10019

ᴀVON ⬟ GOTHIC ORIGINALS
ᴍASTERPIECES OF SUSPENSE!

Crucible of Evil   Lyda Belknap Long

Amanda Lescot left her childhood home, Lescot Manor Hall, to escape an evil too horrible to be borne. But in a sudden flash of mysterious and terrifying circumstances, her sinister ordeal began again—leading to a fearsome struggle to overcome dark and mysterious forces!

(19646—95¢)

The Spirit of Brynmaster Oaks
Anne J. Griffin

A beautiful young bride learns of her husband's sinister past—and the terrifying vision that will come to haunt them both—as they are plunged into a strange web of suffocating evil!   (19737—95¢)

Stark Island   Lynna Cooper

Inez came to Stark House to catalogue the library, but one night as she took a moonlight swim in Deepdene Pool, she saw a pair of bright eyes watching her from the shrubbery. Thus began her encounter with a horrible creature, and a macabre figure in the family mausoleum!   (19463—95¢)

Where better paperbacks are sold, or directly from the publisher. Include 25¢ per copy for mailing; allow three weeks for delivery.

Avon Books, Mail Order Dept., 250 West 55th Street, New York, N. Y. 10019